Dear Mum, You're Ruining My Life

Jean Van Leeuwen has had a number of children's novels published in America, as well as a series of Easy-to-Read books for younger children that have also been published in the UK.

She lives with her husband and two children in Chappaqua, New York.

D1391010

Jean Van Leeuwen

DEAR MUM, YOU'RE RUINING MY LIFE

Piper Books
PAN MACMILLAN
CHILDREN'S BOOKS

First published in Great Britain 1990 by
Macmillan Children's Books,
a division of Macmillan Publishers Ltd
This Piper edition published 1991 by
Pan Macmillan Children's Books,
a division of Pan Macmillan Limited
Cavaye Place, London SW10 9PG

5 7 9 8 6 4

© Jean Van Leeuwen 1988

The right of the author to be identified as author of this work
has been asserted by her in accordance with the Copyright, Designs
and Patents Act 1988.

ISBN 0 330 31986 8

Printed in England by Clays Ltd, St Ives plc

For my daughter Elizabeth,
who has filled my mailbox with
many memorable notes

One

Dear Mr Tooth Fairy,

Please come to Samantha Slayton's house tonight, 14 Mayberry Road, West Greenbush, NY. There is a tooth waiting for you there.

Sincerely,
Samantha Slayton

In Sam's house her father was the tooth fairy. Her mother used to be, but she wasn't very good at it. She tended to forget. That was because she was a writer, and when she was working on a poem or a story, her mind drifted. Most of the time Sam didn't mind her mother being absent-minded, but when in second grade the same tooth lay under her pillow for four nights without turning into money, she had cried. After that her father had taken over the tooth-fairy job.

Her father was an excellent tooth fairy. He hardly ever forgot, and he paid better than her mother had: fifty cents a tooth. And he left funny notes under her pillow along with the money, written in teeny fairylike handwriting.

There was one strange thing about her father as the tooth fairy, though. He saved the teeth. And he wasn't a dentist either, he was a mathematician. Her father just liked to save things, especially things that Sam or her older brother Bradley had made. Sam's mother claimed that he had even saved Bradley's umbilical cord when he was born. Sam hoped her mother was just joking. But she had the sinking feeling that probably her father did have Bradley's thirteen-year-old umbilical cord filed away somewhere in one of the tall filing cabinets in his study. Under *U* for umbilical, or maybe *B* for belly button.

Sam hadn't given the tooth fairy any business for quite a while. But now, a week before she was going to start sixth grade, she suddenly had a loose tooth.

She first discovered it on the night of the corn-eating contest. They were all having dinner at the picnic table in the back yard. Her father had grilled hamburgers. Her mother had cooked corn on the cob, Sam's absolute favourite food. They were on their third ear, butter dripping from chins, a pile of empty cobs growing in the middle of the table, when Sam noticed something odd about her father.

"Dad," she said, "how come you eat your corn in that funny way?"

Her father stopped eating. "What funny way?"

"You know. Around in a circle."

Sam ate hers from side to side. So did Bradley and her mother. She thought everyone did.

"Extremely strange," pronounced Bradley. According to him everything his parents did was strange. Sam thought he was the strange one, with his hair covering his eyes like a sheepdog's, his black T-shirts with pictures of weird rock groups, and – his most

2

recent addition – a New York Mets baseball cap, which he wore back to front.

"I think my method is more efficient," said her father. "It's one continuous motion, you see. No wasted energy."

"Side to side is more efficient," Bradley said positively. He would argue with anyone about anything. "No wasted energy twirling."

Sam's father smiled. "There's one way to find out. I challenge all of you to a corn-eating contest. Winner gets the last ear of corn."

"I can't eat another bite," said Sam's mother. But she volunteered to referee the contest.

"No fair skipping kernels," she said. "I'll check your cobs. Are you ready? Get set. Eat!"

Sam, her father, and Bradley started chewing.

Around and around went her father.

From side to side went Sam, eating three rows at a time.

She glanced over at her father. He was twirling and chewing like an eating machine. She could barely see Bradley behind his hair. But his mouth was moving fast.

Sam ate faster. But her swallowing wasn't keeping up with her chewing. Her cheeks were full of mushed-up corn.

Her father was almost finished. Sam couldn't believe it. Where did he put all that corn? But so was Bradley. He was a mess. Corn was stuck to his cheeks, in his hair, on the end of his nose.

Sam swallowed and started another row. Just then she felt something inside her mouth bend.

"I win!" exclaimed Bradley triumphantly.

"Well," said her father, "only by a mouthful. I think all it proves is that you have younger jaws."

"What's the matter, Sam?" asked her mother.

Sam felt around until she found it. "My tooth," she said in surprise. "It's loose."

"Must be a twelve-year molar," said her mother.

"But I'm not even eleven yet."

Her mother smiled. "You always did do everything early."

Sam wiggled the tooth with her finger. It seemed very loose.

"Why don't we just pull it out?" suggested her mother.

Sam wasn't sure. If her mother or father pulled out the tooth, it would hurt and bleed. The sight of blood made her sick to her stomach. On the other hand, if she waited for it to fall out by itself, the corn season would probably be over. Also it might fall out in school.

"Step into my office," invited her father, putting down his corn cob to twirl an imaginary moustache. "This will only take a moment, heh, heh, heh."

Bradley attempted to make a muscle with his skinny stringbean arm. "I could do it in thirty seconds," he said, waving his fist in the air.

Sam shuddered. "No thanks," she said to all of them.

For the next few days Sam had no corn on the cob. No steak cooked on the grill. No delicious peaches, plums, or nectarines. While the rest of the family chewed away on her summer favourites with

4

their firmly attached teeth, her dinners consisted of peanut-butter sandwiches and ice cream. Sam liked peanut butter and she loved ice cream, but she was getting tired of them.

On the night before the first day of school, Sam sat on her bed in her tiny room at the top of the house, surrounded by her animals. At last count there were thirty-three of them, all stuffed. Eight of them slept on her bed. It was a little crowded, but Sam liked being crowded by her animals. It felt cosy.

She held her mirror up to her mouth. With the tip of her tongue she wiggled her loose tooth. It felt looser than it had before dinner. Sam frowned. She still couldn't decide whether it would be worse to spit blood into the sink or have the tooth come out during lunch in the cafeteria, or maybe in class with a new teacher. As usual when she couldn't decide something, she called her friend Katy on the phone.

The telephone rang five times and no one answered. Sam knew Katy's family was home. Where else would anyone be the night before school started? But sometimes they didn't answer their phone, if they were playing family string quartets or having an interesting conversation or if they just didn't feel like it. They were that kind of family.

Sam let it ring two more times.

"Hello?" said Katy.

"Hi. It's me. What's new?"

"Nothing much," said Katy. "My cat caught a chipmunk and brought it to the dining room while we were having dinner."

Sam's stomach lurched. Quickly she changed the subject. "Did you decide what you're wearing to school tomorrow?"

"My overalls and a shirt, I guess."

"Which shirt?"

"I don't know. Whichever one is clean."

It wasn't very satisfying having a conversation with Katy about clothes. She didn't care what she wore.

"I can't decide between my pink shirt and my lavender," Sam said. "The lavender matches my new nail polish. But the pink matches my hot-pink socks."

Katy didn't say anything. If she didn't have anything to say, she kept quiet. Sam liked that about her.

"I still don't know what to do about my tooth," Sam went on. "My father says it's hanging by a thread."

"Pull it out," advised Katy.

"Myself?"

"Sure."

Katy could do that. She didn't care about blood. She thought it was interesting, like mould on bread and dead chipmunks that her cat brought to the dining-room table. Katy was considering being a doctor when she grew up.

"I can't do that," Sam told her. "I'd get sick."

Katy didn't answer. Sam imagined her shrugging her shoulders on the other end of the phone.

"You really think I should get it pulled out?"

"Either that or wear your pink shirt tomorrow."

"Why the pink?"

6

"So the blood won't show."

"So long," said Sam hastily. "See you in school."

"So long," said Katy.

Sam gathered together her three favourite stuffed animals, the rabbit sisters, for courage, and went to find her mother.

She was in her bedroom with her feet up, reading the newspaper. She looked up warily. "Please don't require any services," she said. "I just sat down for the first time since breakfast."

"You don't have to get up," Sam assured her. "I just want to talk to you. About my tooth."

Her mother sighed and put down her newspaper.

Sam and her rabbits sat in the other chair. "Well," she said. "I *think* I want it out before I go to school. But what if it isn't ready to come out? What if it won't stop bleeding? I might die from loss of blood."

Her mother smiled. "One little tooth isn't going to cause massive bleeding. You'll wash out your mouth and that will be it."

Sam wasn't completely convinced. Parents had a way of making terrible things sound like nothing at all. Just a tiny teaspoon of medicine. It can't taste bad, it's pink. Just a few mushrooms in the sauce. You won't even know they are there. Sam would always know when a mushroom was there.

"But what if you try to pull it and it won't come out?"

"Open your mouth," said her mother.

Sam did.

"Wiggle it."

Sam poked the tooth with her tongue.

"It's ready."

Sam's stomach turned inside out.

"Don't worry, Sam." Her mother smiled encouragingly. "That tooth is waving in the breeze. All we have to do is reach in and yank it out."

Sam wished she hadn't used that word. But she followed her mother down the hall to the bathroom, clutching Sally, her favourite rabbit.

Sam's mother turned on the bright fluorescent light. She arranged Sam on a stool. The bathroom began to feel like an operating room.

"Is this the tooth?" her mother asked.

"Don't touch it!"

Her mother jumped back as if she'd been burned. "Why?"

"I'm not ready yet."

Sam's mother rolled her eyes at the ceiling. "I was sitting in my room having a nice read, under the impression that I'd got through another day. Why me? Why not your father? He does excellent tooth-fairy work. I'm sure he could handle an extraction equally efficiently."

"I'm afraid he might be *too* efficient," Sam said.

"Mmm. Oh, yes, the moustache-twirling. Not exactly a confidence builder, I guess."

"You're more patient. And kind."

Her mother smiled. "Well, I think I'm more patient and kind earlier in the day, but I'll try. I'll tell you what. You let me know when you're ready. Then we'll do it very fast."

Sam took a deep breath. For the last time she

touched the loose tooth with her tongue. In a minute it would be gone.

"Ready."

Her mother leaned forward, a tissue in her hand. Sam thought of blood.

"Not ready."

"Sam! You promised."

"I'm sorry. I'll try again." Sam closed her eyes. She tried to think peaceful thoughts. Puffy white clouds. Deep-blue seas. Rainbows. She opened her eyes.

"Ready."

The hand with the tissue approached. Sam squeezed Sally hard. That reminded her of something.

"Wait."

"What is it?" Her mother looked as if being patient and kind was getting to be hard work.

"If I die, give all my animals to Katy. Except Sally. I want her buried with me. Oh, and tell Mr O'Malley I'm sorry I couldn't be on the soccer team."

Her mother nodded.

"And don't give Bradley any of my things."

"Got it," said her mother grimly.

"Okay," said Sam. "I'm ready."

The hand reached into her mouth. She felt it grasp the tooth. The tissue draped over her tongue like a soggy blanket, choking her.

Stop! Wait! Not ready! Sam was yelling inside her head. But it was too late.

"Well, what do you know?" Her mother seemed surprised. She held out a crumpled tissue. In the middle of it, small, white, and harmless-looking lay Sam's tooth.

Sam hadn't felt a thing. But there was a hole in her mouth as wide as the Grand Canyon. And she tasted blood.

"Is it bleeding?" she asked.

"Not too profusely," her mother said.

Sam rinsed out her mouth. Bright red blood spattered the sides of the sink. Revolting. She rinsed again. More blood. Disgusting. Sam rinsed seven more times. Finally the water she spat into the sink wasn't pink.

"That wasn't so bad, was it?" her mother asked.

Sam thought she was probably about to faint from loss of blood. "It was terrible," she said.

"Well, anyway, that's one molar down, two to go. Or is it three?"

"Actually," said Sam, "I think the school nurse said there are eight."

"Eight," repeated her mother. "I see. And do you expect to have a nervous breakdown each time?"

"Probably," said Sam.

"Oh," said her mother. "Excuse me. I think I'll go lie down. Suddenly I'm feeling rather tired."

She handed Sam a tiny package of folded tissue. "Here you are. All ready for delivery to the tooth fairy."

"Thanks," said Sam.

Dear Ms Slayton,

We at Tooth Fairy Enterprises have rarely seen such a fine specimen of molar as the one found beneath your pillow this evening. In consideration of this fact, and of your courage in the face of extraction, we are pleased to pay you (on a one-time-only basis) at a rate of fifty per cent higher than the usual fee.

Your faithful servant,
T. Fairy

Two

Dear Katy,

What do you think of Mr Speigel? I never knew science was like this. Did he really change water into wine? I think his beard is weird. He reminds me of a bear (grizzly).

Sixth grade is so different. The best thing so far is study hall. Maybe we can get our homework done in school. The worst things are: changing rooms all the time, two hours of homework a night (Mrs Pinkney must be kidding), and late lunch.

Do you like Bonnie and Betsy's Ash Cans? I think it's dumb to dress like twins when you're not. Write back.

Love,
Sam

Sam was a person with many worries. She had noticed this about herself lately, and it worried her. Maybe she was getting like her grandma Wheeler.

Grandma Wheeler worried about things that never even crossed the minds of most people. Like what if lightning were to strike the TV aerial during a thunderstorm? It could travel down the wires and electrocute you while you were switching channels. Or what if the dog had licked the rattle that the baby was now putting in her mouth? She might get distemper or worms or even rabies. Or what if that tiny rattling noise under the hood was something wrong with the carburettor? The car would break down and no petrol stations would be open because it was a holiday and they'd be late for Thanksgiving dinner and how would Aunt Betty keep the turkey warm?

It was probably inevitable that Sam would grow up to be a worrier. She had worry genes from both sides of her family. Her father was also a skilled worrier. Only he worried about different things: nuclear waste, food additives, the Middle East, the future of the mathematical sciences in the age of the computer, the balance in his bank account at the end of the month. He specialised in big worries.

Sam's worries weren't exactly big. But there were a lot of them. As she walked to the bus stop on the first morning of sixth grade, she felt them hanging over her like a dark, damp cloud.

There was her height (five feet five and a half and growing). Last year she'd been the second-tallest kid in her class, next to Jimmy Humphrey. Sam was worried that this year she might be the tallest. Maybe even the tallest kid in the whole school. And her feet (size eight and growing). What if they never stopped? By seventh grade she could outgrow women's sizes and only be able to fit into men's basketball shoes. And her bra. Her mother had insisted on buying it for her over the summer. Should she wear it to school? Would anyone else be wearing one? Sam did not want to be the first girl in the sixth grade to wear a bra.

Then there was the problem of clothes in general. Was her outfit okay, or would all the other girls be wearing some style she didn't know about? And the sixth-grade teachers. Were they really as mean as everyone said? And her friend Rebecca. Would they be friends this year like they'd been in fourth grade or enemies like in fifth?

These thoughts were swirling around in Sam's head as she got to the bus stop. She was the biggest kid there, she saw immediately. She'd known she would be, since Marcy Atwood from across the street now rode the junior high bus. Still it felt odd standing there with seven little kids, towering over them like a mother hen with a flock of chicks. They were all dressed in their first-day-of-school clothes, bubbling with excitement, obviously not worried about a thing. Sam remembered when she used to feel that way. It hadn't been so long ago.

"Well, Samantha, did you have a good summer? My, aren't you getting to be quite a young lady!" It was Mrs Mattingly, the mother of a second-grade boy.

Sam didn't know what to say. If she opened her mouth, she thought she might cluck. Instead she smiled weakly. Good grief. This year she was even taller than Mrs Mattingly.

It was a relief when the school bus rumbled around the corner. It was an even bigger relief to see Rebecca sitting in the first seat.

"Hi." Sam plopped down beside her.

"Hi." Rebecca smiled. Sam couldn't tell if it was a let's-be-friends-this-year smile or a thank-goodness-now-I-have-someone-to-sit-with-besides-little-kids smile.

"How was Martha's Vineyard?" Sam asked her.

"Fantastic. How was Long Lake?"

"Terrific." Actually it had been boring. It had rained almost every day and there was nothing to do. Her mother and father had read books and talked about how great the air was and Bradley had gone fishing.

"I met a cute boy," said Rebecca. "His family had the house next to ours. His name was Michael."

While Rebecca talked about Michael, who looked exactly like the movie star Matt Moon, even though he was only thirteen, Sam checked out her clothes. Rebecca was not wearing a bra. Sam could tell: no shoulder straps. She had on plain white socks, all baggy and falling down. Either she'd put on her father's jogging socks by mistake or this was a new style. Sam crossed her legs, trying to cover her hot-pink socks. Last spring everyone had been wearing them. Maybe today no one would. And Rebecca was wearing new jeans. Not just any new jeans, but Funky Dogs. They were the latest style. Sam had seen a TV commercial for them just this morning at breakfast. She thought they looked terrific. Her parents hadn't seemed impressed though. Her mother had remarked that she was glad to see that the bleached-out patched jeans she'd had ever since college were finally in style. And her father had said that in his day if you were a dog, you didn't advertise it on your back pocket. Her parents weren't exactly into fashion.

"Where did you get your jeans?" she asked Rebecca.

"The Denim Barn. They cost a fortune. I had to use some of my birthday money, but it's worth it. Guess who I saw at the Denim Barn?"

15

"Who?"

"Eric Johnson. And he looks even cuter than last year. His hair got blonder over the summer. Oh, I wish he was in our class."

Maybe she and Rebecca wouldn't be friends this year, Sam thought. So far all she had talked about was clothes and boys. Sam was kind of interested in clothes and a little bit interested in boys, but she didn't want to talk about them all the time. It got boring.

It was a relief to get off the bus and see Katy standing there chewing on a long blade of grass. She was wearing one of her normal Katy outfits: paint-splashed overalls that had once belonged to her older brother and a striped dress shirt of her father's with the sleeves rolled up. Katy never went clothes-shopping. She just wore leftovers from the rest of her family.

"Don't you think it's weird," she said, frowning, "that grass is always the same shape? You never see round grass or oblong grass. It's always long and thin."

"That's why it's called a blade," Sam said.

"Hey, that's right!" Only Katy could be thinking about blades of grass on the first morning of sixth grade. Sam was glad to see her.

They walked together through the crowded, noisy hallway and up the stairs to Mrs Pinkney's room. Sam and Katy found seats together near the window. Hardly anyone was there yet, not even the teacher.

"Good, I can finish my book," said Katy, digging out a science-fiction paperback from her knapsack.

Sam looked over the other kids as they arrived.

Jimmy Humphrey was bigger than ever, she was glad to see. He was built like a melon. She and he might be tied for tallest sixth-grader, but he was definitely the *biggest*. Sam checked all the girls for shoulder straps, but she couldn't detect any. Thank goodness her bra was safely at home in her bottom drawer. Droopy white socks were definitely in style. So were Funky Dogs. Sara Hersheiser had them, naturally. She did everything Rebecca did. And Heather Horowitz and her friend Meredith. And Susie Ling. It was beginning to look as if Sam and Katy were the only girls without a dog embroidered on their back pockets.

Bonnie Carpenter and Betsy Stearns hadn't come in yet. They were the ones Sam was waiting for. They had been the first girls to get their ears pierced, back in fourth grade. They'd also been the first to wear purple nail polish, in fifth grade. Whatever you were supposed to be wearing in sixth grade, Bonnie and Betsy would be wearing it.

Everyone was seated and Mrs Pinkney was about to close the door when they dashed in, giggling.

"Will you two ladies find seats so we can begin?"

The teacher's voice was stern. Bonnie and Betsy stopped giggling and sat down.

Sam glanced over at them. They were dressed exactly alike. The Bobbsey Twins, Sam always called them to herself. They didn't look alike – Bonnie had long dark hair and Betsy was blonde – but everything else about them was the same. Surprisingly, they were not wearing Funky Dogs, but a different kind of jeans. These jeans were even more worn-out looking, and instead of faded blue they were faded grey. Sam had seen them on TV too. They were called Ash Cans.

With them Bonnie and Betsy wore sweatshirts with the sleeves cut off, droopy white socks, and dangling, heart-shaped earrings. And they both were carrying makeup bags.

Oh, no. Not makeup too. Sam couldn't stand it. Her mother wouldn't let her wear makeup until she graduated from high school.

Suddenly Sam felt like crawling under her desk. Everything she was wearing was wrong. Boring regular jeans, an uncut-up shirt, no earrings, no makeup bag, no makeup. And worst of all, hot-pink socks.

She could raise her hand and ask to go to the girls' room. She'd take off the socks and throw them in the rubbish bin. No socks would be better than awful hot-pink ones.

Sam stole another look at Bonnie. She was taking a pencil out of her makeup bag. Not an eyebrow pencil, a regular yellow one. That was strange. Then all at once Sam understood. Makeup bags were what sixth-graders were going to be carrying their pencils in this year.

While she was in the girls' room she'd get rid of her babyish rabbit pencil case too.

Sam started to raise her hand. But then she noticed that Mrs Pinkney was talking.

"I suspect you're all wondering what sixth grade will be like," she said in a soft, serious voice. "Well, it's going to be different."

Sam listened as she explained about changing classrooms for maths and science, and having a study hall at the end of the day, and what they would be learning in English and social studies. Switching classrooms seemed confusing and the work sounded hard. But Mrs Pinkney made it sound as if they could handle it. And she actually smiled. Sam didn't think she was mean at all.

Mr Puccio, the maths teacher, didn't seem mean either. He was strict about kids talking, and he was very serious about maths. But Sam didn't mind. Maths was one of her best subjects.

It was the science teacher, Mr Speigel, though, who was the big surprise. He was very large and very hairy, with a walrus moustache and a shaggy brown beard. Standing in the science lab, surrounded by test tubes and Bunsen burners, he looked like an evil scientist from a horror movie. But then he began to talk.

He talked about what science was, and how people do scientific experiments in their everyday lives without even knowing it. And while he was talking, he was lining up four test tubes in front of him. He said he was performing a scientific experiment right now. He was trying to see if he could turn water into wine. And while everyone watched, the water actually turned pink and then dark pink and then red as he poured it from one test tube to another. No one could believe it. Even Marshall Tucker seemed puzzled. He thought he knew everything, and always had his hand waving in the air. Katy called him the Human Brain.

But then Mr Speigel stopped pouring. "Oh, my, I forgot. Your parents probably wouldn't approve of my having wine in the classroom. I'd better change it back to water."

And he poured it back from the last test tube to the first, and it got lighter and lighter until finally it was perfectly clear again, like pure water.

19

"How did you do that?"

"That wasn't really wine, was it?"

They were all talking at once, without even raising their hands.

Mr Speigel looked delighted. "How do *you* think I did it? You're all scientists. See if you can figure it out."

Everyone started offering ideas, crazy ones and sensible ones. A lot had to do with dye.

Jimmy Humphrey asked, "Is it a magic trick?"

Mr Speigel laughed. "In a way, yes. It's the magic of chemistry."

Sam didn't say anything. She was feeling kind of strange. She wasn't used to having a teacher like this. She glanced over at Katy. Katy looked the way Sam felt. She was staring at Mr Speigel with her mouth hanging open.

Sam was startled when the bell rang. It couldn't be the end of class already. And then, just as she was walking out of the door of Mr Speigel's room, something else surprising happened.

She bumped into Brian Finnegan. Brian Finnegan of the million freckles and the million jokes. Brian Finnegan, who had once stolen her lunch box, eaten everything he liked, and thrown the rest up a tree. Brian Finnegan, whom she had known since nursery school.

"Hey, watch it, Slayton," he said with a grin.

Brian Finnegan had the cutest grin. Somehow she'd never noticed it before.

Suddenly Sam stopped breathing. Her face felt hot, as if it were on fire. Her hands felt cold. What was going on here? Was she coming down with a fever? Or could this be what it felt like to like a boy?

Mrs Pinkney was right, Sam thought. Sixth grade was going to be very different.

Dear Sam,

I think Mr Speigel is the greatest teacher. It wasn't water or wine, I bet. Probably some kind of chemicals. I like beards, especially brown bushy ones. My father's reminds me of a goat's all black and white. He says we are responsible for the white (his kids, get it?). Bonnie and Betsy's jeans look like they came from an ash can. I have decided to do scientific research when I grow up.

Love,
Katy

Three

PROBLEM: *TO GO TO DANCING CLASS*
OR NOT?

Reasons to go
  1. You have to know how to dance when
     you grow up.
  2. Everyone else is going.
  3. Brian Finnegan is going.

Reasons not to go
  1. Dancing looks dumb.
  2. I was bad when I took ballet.
  3. I will probably step on all the boys' feet.
  4. The boys are all short.
  5. You have to get dressed up.
  6. You have to wear white gloves.

SOLUTION: *I shouldn't sign up for dancing*
class.

Well, thought Sam, that was it. She'd used the
method of logical decision-making that her father
always recommended, and it had come out 6–3 against
the Monday-night dancing class at the Community
Centre. She wasn't going. She would call Rebecca
and tell her.

But what if it turned out that Sam was the

22

only one who didn't? On Tuesday mornings everyone would be talking about dancing class and she would feel left out.

Well, she wouldn't be the *only* one. Katy wasn't going. She hated dresses, she said, and she refused to buy one. And a few of the boys weren't. The ones Rebecca called geeks.

But what about Brian Finnegan? If she didn't go, she would never have a chance to dance with him.

But if she did go, she might dance with him and step on his feet.

Sam was all confused. She put away her logical-decision-making list and went to find her mother.

She was standing at the kitchen stove, stirring a pan of pudding and listening to her favourite sickening love songs on the radio. Her mother had terrible taste in music.

"Uh – Mum?" Sam said.

"Uh – yes?"

"When you were my age, did you go to dancing class?"

Her mother smiled. "I certainly did. Patent leather shoes and white gloves. The boys had to bow and the girls had to curtsey. It was one of the most awful experiences of my life."

"Oh," said Sam. "I guess I shouldn't go then."

"Well . . . " Her mother hesitated. "Awful things are sometimes worthwhile in the end. It's useful to know how to dance."

"You and Dad don't dance."

"Not regularly, no. Still, every once in a while the occasion arises. Remember your uncle Bob's wedding?"

Her parents had danced a lot that night. Her father had even lifted Sam up and held her against his smooth white dinner jacket, pretending to dance with her. "That was five years ago."

"Then there was the Mathematical Society dinner dance, about ten years ago. I'd say the ability to dance comes in handy about once every five years."

That wasn't much. Probably it wasn't worth it. Sam thought.

"Actually I like to dance," her mother said. "You might like it too. Why don't we give it a try?" Suddenly her mother was on her feet, holding out her arms. The radio was playing a slow song, something about fog and London.

Sam stood up.

Her mother was the right height for dancing, just a little taller than Sam. Not like the boys at school. She would tower over them like a skyscraper. The Empire State Building, one of them had called her last year.

"Feel the beat of the music," her mother said. "And move with it. *One, two, three. One, two, three.*"

Sam couldn't feel the beat of the music. Her legs were stiff like broomsticks. Her foot came down on top of her mother's.

She stopped. "I can't do it," she said. "I'll step on all the boys' feet."

"Maybe they'll step on yours," replied her mother. "Everyone's just learning. Let's try again."

The song had switched. This one had more of a beat. Her mother showed Sam how to move her feet in sort of a box shape.

"*Step, together, glide,*" she chanted. "Feel the music as you go."

Sam thought she was starting to feel the music. Her feet glided across the lino floor.

"Much better," said her mother.

She steered Sam around the round oak table. "*Step, together, glide, turn*. Terrific!"

"*Step, together, glide, turn,*" Sam repeated to herself.

And then, somehow, she did it. Gliding past a chair she bumped her shin. She reached out to steady herself on the wood-burning stove and tripped over her own feet. Sam clutched frantically at her mother, but nothing could save her. She sat down hard on a pile of logs in the woodbox.

"Are you all right?" her mother asked.

Sam rubbed her elbow. "I'll never learn how to dance," she groaned. "I'm a hopeless case."

"There are no hopeless cases," her mother said.

"Ha," said Sam.

Still, when Rebecca called after dinner, Sam told her, "I've decided. I'm going to sign up for dancing class."

Rebecca's mother was driving the first night. Rebecca had arranged a complicated car pool including everyone from their section of town. Bonnie was in it, and Sara, and even two boys. Mark Hartigan and Jimmy Humphrey. No Brian Finnegan, though. He lived in a different area.

Sam was being picked up at seven-fifteen. At six forty-five she went into the bathroom with everything she was going to need: her skirt and new lace blouse, her black fancy shoes, her tights still in their cellophane wrapper, five of her collection of heart necklaces to see which looked best, two bracelets, the perfume Grandma Wheeler had brought her from Hawaii, her comb, brush, and curling iron.

First she unwrapped the tights. She'd never worn tights before. They looked fragile. What if she got a ladder while she was dancing? What if she got a ladder just putting them on? Sam carefully put one foot in. She smoothed them over her ankle, then put the other foot in. Slowly she worked them up her legs. Looking down, Sam was amazed. Her legs looked all grown up.

"Are you ever coming out? I need to use the bathroom."

It was Bradley.

"Go away," said Sam.

"Why should I? It's my bathroom too."

Sam heard her mother calling Bradley.

"Jerk," he muttered. His feet clumped down the stairs.

Next Sam put on her blouse and skirt. She tried on all the heart necklaces. The blue one looked best, she decided. She dabbed perfume behind her ears and on her wrists, as she'd seen her mother do.

"Are you ready, Sam?"

It was her mother this time.

"Almost," said Sam.

"You're wearing your bra, aren't you? You'll need it with that blouse."

Sam looked in the mirror. Maybe her mother was right. But she didn't want to wear her bra. Worrying about shoulder straps at the same time she would be worrying about stepping on boys' feet was more than she could cope with.

"Do you need any help?"

"No!" said Sam, alarmed. "I'll be down soon."

As soon as her mother left, Sam dashed to her room. Where was her bra anyway? She finally found it in her bottom drawer. And there was the slip Aunt Linda had given her last Christmas. Better wear it too.

Sam raced back to the bathroom. She struggled into the bra, then the slip. It was pretty: white with pink rosebuds dotted all over it. Sam was beginning to feel like her mother, wearing all this underwear.

She finished dressing and looked in the mirror again. Oh, no. You could see the rosebuds through the blouse. She looked as if she were sprinkled with pink dots.

"Sam, it's ten past seven."

Suddenly Sam felt tears welling up in her eyes.

"I'm not going," she mumbled, sniffing.

"What's wrong?" asked her mother.

Sam didn't answer.

The doorknob rattled. "Sam, I'm coming in."

Sam turned her back so her mother wouldn't see that she was crying. But her mother saw.

"Oh, Sam," she said, and put her arms around her.

For a minute they just stood there. Her mother hugged Sam. Sam sniffed.

"Now," said her mother. "Tell me about the problem."

Sam pointed to her chest. "It's the rosebuds," she whispered. "You can see them through the blouse."

Her mother looked closer. "I see what you mean," she said. "But, Sam, the lights at the Community

27

Centre will be dim. And no one will be trying to look through your blouse. No one is going to see the rosebuds, I promise."

Sam stared into the mirror. Besides the rosebuds, her hair was standing on end, as out of control on the outside as Sam felt on the inside. And now her eyes were puffy and her nose looked like a light bulb.

A car honked in the driveway.

"Oh, no!" moaned Sam. "I can't go like this. What am I going to do?"

Sam's mother ran cold water in the sink. "Here's what you're going to do. First wash your face. Then get your jacket and go out there. It will be dark when you get in the car. By the time you get to the Community Centre you'll look fine."

Sam hesitated. "But what about the rosebuds?"

"Don't think about them any more. Really, Sam."

Sam knew what she was going to do about the rosebuds. She was going to keep her jacket on the entire time she was at dancing class.

It was dark in the car. No one could see Sam's puffy eyes. She was squeezed in next to Jimmy Humphrey, who took up a lot of room and smelled like soap. There was the smell of mixed perfumes in the car. And the rustle of skirts. But except for the crunch of gravel under the tyres, that was the only sound. No one was saying anything.

It was strange. Usually Rebecca talked all the time. And Jimmy Humphrey had always been a big talker, constantly making dumb jokes. He kept clearing his throat, but no jokes came out.

It seemed like a long drive to the Community

Centre. Sam concentrated on not touching Jimmy Humphrey. It wasn't easy when they turned corners. She pressed herself against the car door, hoping the lock wouldn't give way and deposit her on the street.

A line of cars was dropping kids off. Everyone *had* signed up for dancing class, it seemed. Not just from their school but the other two elementary schools too.

Suddenly everyone in the car started talking at once. "Thank you," they all said to Rebecca's mother.

Inside the Community Centre it was bright and noisy. Groups of kids stood around. Everyone was dressed up. The boys looked like some entirely different species from the boys Sam knew at school. With their hair combed, wearing jackets and ties, they looked like fathers who'd been put in the washing machine and shrunk.

All except Brian Finnegan. His grey jacket was unbuttoned, his shirt was untucked, and his tie flapped over one shoulder as he pulled Susie Ling's ponytail and ran away laughing.

Sam's stomach did an odd flip-flop. Liking someone made you feel as if you were getting ill all the time, she'd noticed.

She stood in a circle with Rebecca and Sara and Bonnie and Betsy.

"Did you see Eric Johnson?" Rebecca whispered. "He looks *so* good in that blue blazer."

"How about Mark Hartigan in his polka-dot tie?" said Bonnie.

Betsy giggled. "Susie told me that Victoria told her that Peter Phelps told her that Mark likes you."

Sam hadn't said anything to anyone about Brian Finnegan. She wasn't going to, she decided. Secrets didn't seem to be secrets any more in sixth grade. If Brian Finnegan found out she liked him, Sam would die.

Two mothers were standing at the door of the gym. "Hang your jackets here," one said, "and you can go inside."

There was no choice. Sam took off her jacket. There went the rosebud plan.

She didn't have time to think about the rosebuds anyway. In the gym the girls had to sit on chairs lined up on one side of the room. The boys sat on the other side. In the middle stood the dancing teacher, a man with slicked-back blond hair, wearing a blue blazer and red-striped tie.

"My name is Mr Dunphy," he announced with a smile that Sam instantly decided was phoney. "And I am going to teach you to dance."

A low groan came from the boys' side of the room.

Mr Dunphy went on, relentlessly smiling. "Some of you may not believe it, but by the end of tonight's class you'll be dancing. And we're going to have fun doing it. We'll play some good music – a little rock, a little disco. All you have to do is relax and have fun. So let's get started."

Everyone stood up.

"Now, boys," Mr Dunphy said, "each of you is going to invite a girl to dance."

Sam looked over the boys lined up opposite her. They were all short. The boys from the other schools were unfortunately the same size as the ones from her school. Only Jimmy Humphrey and a dark-haired boy with glasses looked almost her size.

"You are going to do it politely," Mr Dunphy

went on. "You will walk up to a girl and say, 'Would you care to dance?' And, girls, you will say yes, just as politely and walk with your partner to the dance floor."

Maybe Brian Finnegan would ask her to dance. No, not her. Not the Empire State Building. Anyway, if by any chance he did, she would trample him with her giant feet. Or trip over her giant feet and end up sprawled on the gym floor. Why had she ever signed up for dancing class?

"Boys, you may now invite a young lady to dance."

A stampede of boys poured across the floor. Three of them arrived at the same time in front of Bonnie. "Care to dance?" they all asked. Bonnie gave them each a dazzling smile. "Yes," she said to a freckled redheaded boy. The other two scurried away.

On the other side of Sam, two boys invited Rebecca to dance.

Now Sam was standing alone, except for Heather Horowitz. Brian Finnegan had asked Susie Ling to dance, she saw. Boys were darting from one short girl to another.

Maybe there weren't enough boys to go around. Maybe Sam and Heather would have to dance together. She couldn't do it. It would be too embarrassing.

A blond boy who looked exhausted from running all over the gym suddenly appeared in front of Sam. He was about two feet tall and looked no more than eight years old. "Care to dance?" he mumbled, looking at the floor.

"Oh," stammered Sam. "Uh – okay."

They danced. Sort of. Mr Dunphy demonstrated

how to do the box step, which Sam recognised from her lesson with her mother. It was the basis of all ballroom dancing, he told them. They all stood in one place and made boxes with their feet over and over.

That terrible picture of herself in the woodbox was stuck in Sam's brain. She kept looking down at her feet to make sure they were doing the right thing.

"Look at your partners, boys and girls," urged Mr Dunphy. "Your feet will take care of themselves."

But her feet weren't taking care of themselves. She felt her giant foot come down on the blonde boy's small one. "Sorry," she whispered.

A minute later he kicked her ankle. "Sorry," he mumbled.

After a few minutes Mr Dunphy had them change partners. Sam made boxes with another shrimpy boy, this one wearing a jacket that must have belonged to his older brother. The sleeves covered his hands. Then she danced with Jimmy Humphrey, who stepped on her toe five times. And then they were allowed to sit down and rest.

Mr Dunphy moved out to the middle of the dance floor. With a high school girl as his partner, he demonstrated how they all should look while dancing. "Backs straight. Hands lightly clasped. Boys, it's your job to do the leading. Think of it like driving a car."

Sam didn't like being compared to a car. And she didn't like watching Mr Dunphy and his blonde partner, who didn't step on his foot once and was even able to smile while doing complicated dance steps. Sam would never be able to do that. She was a hopeless case.

The dancing class seemed to go on for ever.

Sam danced with more shrimpy boys. But never with Brian Finnegan. She did hundreds of box steps. She said "Sorry" hundreds of times. Her feet hurt from being stepped on. Her ankle hurt and her head hurt and her arms hurt from holding them in the dancing position.

Finally it was the last dance. Again the boys had to invite the girls. Sam didn't think she could face it, standing there waiting until some worn-out boy who'd been defeated in his first six choices grudgingly asked her to dance. And Bonnie was next to her again too.

"All right, boys," said Mr Dunphy, smiling in a conspiratorial way. That was the signal for the race to begin.

Five boys skidded to a stop in front of Bonnie.

"Would you care to dance?"

Sam couldn't believe it. One of them appeared to be talking to her.

"Y-yes," she managed to say. And she followed him on to the dance floor.

He was short, of course. He had chubby cheeks and strange-looking beige-coloured hair. It stuck up in odd tufts at the back, as if it didn't like being combed. And he was dressed all in beige: tan trousers, tan corduroy jacket, light brown shirt, light brown tie. With orange stripes.

The boy talked while they danced. He asked which school she went to and what was her favourite lunch and did she like sports and, if so, what was her favourite football team.

"Farmingville," said Sam. "Brunch-for-lunch." While she was trying to remember his next question, she stepped on his foot. "Sorry."

"That's okay," said Chubby Cheeks. "What's your favourite subject in school?"

"Uh – science, I guess." Now she'd lost track of her box steps. He stepped on her foot.

"Sorry," he said. "Do you have any hobbies?"

It was no use. Sam couldn't dance and carry on a conversation at the same time. She made a box to the left while Chubby Cheeks was making a box to the right. They bumped into the boy next to them. His feet got tangled up with his partner's.

"Help!" said the boy loudly, waving his arms. "Save me!"

He spun around in a circle, then sat down right in the middle of the dance floor.

It was Brian Finnegan.

Oh, no. How awful. How embarrassing.

"Where am I? How did I get here?" Brian was holding on to his head, but Sam could see him grinning. "This is crazy. I don't dance. Let me out of here!" And he bounced up and walked off the dance floor.

Had Brian noticed that she was the one who had bumped into him? He must think she was clumsy, bumping into him all the time. Well, she was.

She and Chubby Cheeks danced some more. Sam concentrated all her attention on her feet. Chubby Cheeks wouldn't stop talking. He kept asking boring questions, as if he were interviewing her for the evening news. Would this dance ever be over?

And then, finally, the music stopped.

"Thank you for the dance," Chubby Cheeks said politely, smiling at her. "See you next week."

Sam tried to smile back, but her face muscles didn't seem to be working.

"Did you notice?" boomed Mr Dunphy in his jolly voice. "You were all dancing, just as I promised."

Not exactly, thought Sam. With all those boxes they hadn't gone anywhere. Just stayed in one spot, stepping on each other's feet.

"That's it for tonight. See you all next week. And be ready to disco!"

They all went outside to get their jackets.

"Who was that cute red-haired boy?"

"You don't like him? You danced with him five times!"

"Oh, wow, next week we disco."

Bonnie and Betsy and Rebecca and Sara were laughing and talking as they put on their jackets. Everyone seemed to have had a good time. Everyone except Sam. She hurt all over. She could hardly walk. She'd caused an embarrassing scene with Brian Finnegan. And Chubby Cheeks was going to see her next week.

Her mother was right. Dancing class was definitely the most awful experience of her life so far.

PROBLEM: TO GO BACK TO DANCING CLASS OR NOT?

Reasons to go
   1. I can't think of any.

Reasons not to go
   1. Dancing is dumb.
   2. I am as bad at it as I was at ballet.
   3. I will step on all the boys' feet.

4. The boys are all short.
5. You have to get dressed up.
6. You have to wear white gloves.
7. The teacher is a big phoney.
8. Brian Finnegan is going.
9. Chubby Cheeks is going.

SOLUTION: I have to go back.
           My mother is making me.

Four

Dear Mum,

I am working very hard on cleaning my room.
But I want to go to Katy's this afternoon to
work on our Hallowe'en costumes. Can I finish
tomorrow? I would get up early and do it before
breakfast and I'll do a good job. Please? Write
back.

Love,
The Prisoner in the Tower

Dear Prisoner,
No.

Love,
Mum

For days at a time Sam's mother never came up
to her room. And then one day Sam would come
home from school and find the Condemned sign on
her doorknob. Her mother had made the sign. It said:
THIS ROOM IS CONDEMNED. ITS OWNER MAY NOT GO
ANYWHERE OR DO ANYTHING UNTIL THE PREMISES
ARE RESTORED TO NEATNESS. In other words, Sam
was grounded until she cleaned her room.

It wasn't fair. She was always getting the Condemned sign. Bradley hardly ever did. And his room

was really disgusting, with posters of rock stars and basketball stars and movie stars wearing tiny bikinis covering every inch of his walls, and even suspended from the ceiling. But her mother pointed out, his floor was clean. And his desk. That was all she cared about.

Sam had been imprisoned in her room for three hours now. She sat on the floor, looking at everything she was supposed to be putting away. It was possible she might be there all day.

There were her clothes, piled high on her chair and overflowing on to the floor. Assorted shoes. An umbrella from when it rained on Tuesday. Library books. Magazines with pictures of adorable teen movie stars that Rebecca had lent her. Her piano music from yesterday's lesson. And odds and ends of junk: nail-polish remover, cotton balls, a tennis ball, folded-up notes from Katy, rocks from the rock collection they were making for science, pencil stubs, Band-aid wrappers, gum wrappers. And about twenty crumpled tissues.

The thing to do, Sam decided, was sort everything into piles. A pile of dirty laundry, a pile for her dressing-table drawers, a pile to throw away. That was how her father, the organisation man, would do it.

She started with her clothes. The mates to two pairs of socks were missing. Probably under the bed. But she couldn't quite bring herself to look there. She had the sinking feeling that there was as much stuff under the bed as there was on the floor.

She sighed. It was conceivable she could be imprisoned in her room all weekend. She decided to paint her fingernails instead.

Crawling over to the dressing-table she surveyed

38

her nail-polish collection. She had twenty-two shades to choose from. According to her mother they were all awful. But at least she let Sam wear nail polish. Which colour did she feel like wearing today?

Sam had trouble choosing between the frosted pink and bright orange for Hallowe'en. Finally she decided on the orange. Carefully she stroked it on to her left thumb. She thought about going trick-or-treating. She and Katy planned to go in Katy's neighbourhood. And Brian lived only two blocks from Katy. Last year, she remembered, he'd bragged that he'd used up six cans of shaving cream. What if he sprayed her with shaving cream? She wasn't sure if it would be wonderful or awful to get sprayed with shaving cream by Brian Finnegan.

There was a knock on the door.

Sam jumped. "Who is it?" If it was her mother, she was in trouble.

"Brad. I need to talk to you."

"Come in."

Bradley opened the door. Since it had got cooler, he had taken to wearing a limp, faded flannel shirt over his rock-star T-shirts. His hair, which he refused to have cut, now hung down to his nose. And on his head was a crushed brown felt hat which he hadn't taken off for two weeks. Sam's mother said he was making a fashion statement. The only statement he was making to Sam was that he was weird.

He walked over to Sam's mirror. He couldn't pass one these days without sneaking a glance, she'd noticed. On the way he tripped over her umbrella. "Guess you're not making any plans for the weekend, huh, Sam?"

"What do you care?" she retorted. He made her mad, acting like she was the supreme slob and he was perfect. Also, he had on his jacket. Obviously *he* was allowed to go places.

"I don't. I just want to know if I can borrow five dollars. I want to buy a tape in town."

Bradley was always wanting to borrow money from her. He made twice as much as she did, doing baby-sitting and garden work, but she was the one who had money. That was because the only things she spent it on were nail polish and gum.

"Who are you going to town with?" Sam asked.

"Dad. He wants to take a picture of me in front of my Hallowe'en window."

Bradley made a face. That was another thing that made Sam mad. He pretended he didn't care, but she knew secretly he thought he was hot stuff just because he'd won first prize in the Hallowe'en window-painting contest with his gross picture of a dancing skeleton. Bradley was always winning art prizes. Probably he'd be in the newspaper again and her parents would make hundreds of copies to send to their friends and relatives. It was disgusting.

"Why should I lend you more money? You never paid me back the two dollars from last week."

"I did so. I put it on your desk."

"I just cleaned my desk. You never put it there."

"Did so."

"Did not."

Sam was really mad now. He thought she would believe any made-up story he told her. He must think she was stupid.

"Well," said Bradley, putting on his I-am-so-mature-

and- you- are- such- a- big- baby- I- can't- stand- it expression. "Are you going to lend me the money or not?"

"Not!" shouted Sam.

"Okay!" Bradley shouted back. "Be a stupid jerk!" And he pounded down the stairs.

He was the jerk. A lying, conceited, bratty jerk. Sam slammed the door after him. There was something thoroughly satisfying and having-the-last-word about slamming a door.

"Sam!" called her mother. "What's all this yelling and door-slamming about?"

That was just like her mother. She didn't notice Bradley yelling. Oh, no. But she never missed anything Sam did. It must be because she liked Bradley better.

Sam called downstairs, "Nothing!" Then she closed her door, quietly this time.

She picked up her nail polish and started on her middle finger. But she messed it up. Now she would have to take off all the polish and start over.

Instead she got a piece of writing paper. She wrote another letter to her mother.

Dear Gaoler,

You are so mean to me. I have to stay in my room all day while Bradley gets to go to town with Dad. I know you like him better than me. Write back and tell me why you like him better.

The Tower
Prisoner Sam

P.S. Am I your real daughter? I am not joking about this.

41

Silently in her socks Sam padded down to the kitchen.

Her mother was reading a cookery book. "All finished with your room?" she asked, smiling.

Sam stalked over to the fridge and put the letter in the pink construction-paper letter box that was stuck on it with magnets. She had made it when she was eight. Sam put up the red toothpick flag and marched back upstairs.

A minute later her mother knocked on her door.

Sam didn't answer.

"Please let me in, Sam. It's important to talk about your feelings."

Sam said nothing.

There was a long silence. Sam could hear her mother breathing. Finally she sighed. "Well, maybe later."

A few minutes later an envelope poked under the door.

Dear Sam,

I'm sorry you are upset. It's hard to work while other people play. But you don't have to be in there all day. Hurry and finish, and we can make popcorn together.

I don't like Bradley better than you. What makes you think so? Write back and tell me. And of course you are my real daughter. We both have the same beautiful feet, don't we?

Love,
Mum

Beautiful feet — hah! Huge, hideous feet was more like it. And having the same feet didn't prove anything anyway. As her mother was fond of pointing out whenever they went shoe shopping, lots of people had big feet. Famous, glamorous people even, like models and movie stars. So her feet weren't proof she wasn't adopted. Neither was her hair. Everyone said Sam's bushy hair was just like her father's. Sam couldn't understand that, since her father's hair was mostly grey and getting thin on top. But apparently it used to be wild. "It stuck straight up on his head," her grandmother Slayton always used to say. "I couldn't do a thing with it."

So maybe her *real* mother had had big feet and bushy hair. It was possible. Because it was clear to Sam that she didn't belong to this family. All of its other members had some sort of special talent.

Bradley was going to be an artist someday. He could draw anything, and with so much detail that it looked like a photograph. Teachers were always asking him to make posters. And his drawing of the junior high school was so good, it was going to be used on the cover of this year's yearbook. He was practically famous already.

Her father was a maths genius. The research laboratory where he worked paid him just to sit around and think. Sometimes, if he was working on a complicated maths problem, he would keep working on it even after he came home. If you spoke to him, he seemed surprised to find himself in the same room with you. As Bradley said, his light was on but no one was home. Once at night, her mother told them, he had put on his pyjamas, brushed his teeth, taken off his pyjamas, and got dressed to go to work. Sam understood that maths geniuses did things like that. He also played the French horn, very well. Sam played the piano, badly.

And then there was her mother, the writer. Once she had had a job as a magazine editor in New York City. Now she just wrote things: poems, short stories, funny columns that she sent away to newspapers and magazines. Three of her poems had been published in a magazine that her mother said no one but other poets read, and one of her short stories.

What was there about Sam that was special? She was terrible at art. She couldn't carry a tune. In sports she was only so-so. She did well in school, better than Bradley. Only she didn't have any one best subject. Her biggest talent was spelling. In fourth grade she'd won the spelling competition four times, and this year she'd got 100 on every one of Mrs Pinkney's spelling tests so far. But what good was it to be a terrific speller? Maybe when she grew up, she could write dictionaries. That was a bleak thought.

Bleak. That had been one of last week's spelling words. She liked the round, sad sound of it. It summed up her feelings about her room and her family. In fact her whole life.

Sam took out another sheet of writing paper.

Dear Mum,

Okay. Here are the reasons I know you like Bradley better.

1. *He never gets the Condemned sign even though his room is a total mess. If you looked at it sometime, you would agree.*

2. *You are always spending time with him, helping him with his homework. When I ask you for help, you are too busy.*

3. *He gets to stay up later just because he is older even though he has to get up earlier to get the early bus. This is not fair.*

4. *You are always on his side.*

5. *He gets to watch more TV. Sports should count as regular programmes. Anyway, everyone gets to watch more than one hour a day.*

Well, that's it, just the basics. I will not bother you any more with my problems. Just go on with your life and forget about me.

> *Your forgotten daughter,*
> *Sam*

Her mother was putting a casserole in the oven. Sam made a careful detour around her and put the letter in the letter box.

"As long as you're here, would you set the table?" her mother asked quietly.

Sam plopped the place mats down crooked on the table. And she put Bradley's cutlery upside down at his place.

"What's this I see? Can it be that my lovely daughter has emerged from hibernation?"

Her father and Bradley came in the door, smiling, cameras around their necks, eating ice cream cones.

Sam didn't answer.

"Well, we took pictures of the window," her father said. "And Brad and the window, and Brad and the blue ribbon, and Brad and one of the judges. And then I took him out for ice cream to celebrate."

Bradley's cone was chocolate chip mint, Sam noticed. Her favourite flavour. A double scoop.

Suddenly she couldn't stand it. "You just think you're great, don't you? Well, I'll tell you something, Bradley Slayton. You're not great. You're not great at all!"

Sam burst into tears. She started to run from the room, but her father caught her by the shoulders. "Hey, what's all this about?"

Bradley was staring at her, his mouth open. "What did I do? Did I say I was great? I didn't say a word."

"I think we'd all better sit down and have a talk," Sam's mother said quietly.

Sam didn't feel like talking. But her father led her to the kitchen table. She stared down at her crooked place mat while her mother talked.

"Sam has been feeling sad all day. She thinks she is being treated unfairly and that we favour Bradley over her. As I understand it, what bothers her most are the Condemned sign, unequal TV time, and bedtime. Oh, and the amount of help given with homework. Is that right, Sam? Have I covered everything?"

Sam was afraid if she said anything, she might start crying again. She nodded.

"Well, I would just like to say that the homework problem comes as a surprise to me," her mother said. "Bradley asks for help. You hardly ever do, Sam. So I always assumed you could handle it yourself."

It was true she didn't need much help. Still, Sam remembered the time when she really didn't understand latitudes and longitudes and her mother was too busy helping Bradley with alphabetising (which anyone could do) to help her, so she had to ask her father and he explained it in such a complicated way that she'd got all mixed up and got it wrong on the test. She was going to mention that, but she still didn't feel up to talking.

"You don't *need* help," Bradley put in. "Your report card is nothing but A's. Mine is nothing but C's. The only thing I'm good at is art."

Sam looked up, surprised. She didn't know Bradley cared about his grades. She thought all he cared about was art.

He scowled at her. "And what makes you think I have such a great deal with TV? You get to watch any time one of your favourite old movies is on. I never even get to see the second half of *Monday Night Football*. And how about jobs? I have to take out the disgusting rubbish bins, and all you have to do is clean the sink."

Now Bradley was the one who was upset. It sounded as if he had as many things to be angry and upset about as she did.

"The point is, Sam," her father said, "that everyone is different. They need different things. It's not possible for parents to treat children exactly the same. It wouldn't be good for the children. Bradley needs extra help with his schoolwork. You need extra sleep so you can get up for school in the morning."

"And the Condemned sign so you'll clean your room before you trip and break a leg." Sam's mother smiled at her. "We wouldn't want that to happen. Because we love you. Just like we love Bradley. Do you understand, Sam?"

Sam was feeling a little better. Finally she was able to talk. "I guess so," she whispered.

"Good. Now how about finishing up your room? I bet you can do it before dinner."

"I'll try."

Sam went upstairs. She surveyed her floor: the pile of dirty clothes, the shoes, the library books, the scientific rocks, the wall-to-wall scrunched-up tissues. Suddenly she felt very tired.

She gathered all her dirty clothes and dumped them in the laundry basket. She stuffed the clean ones in her drawers. That was a start. Then she sat in the middle of the floor and started tossing junk in the direction of her waste-paper basket. Hit. Miss. Miss. Miss. She'd never be good in basketball.

From far away she heard the tinkle of the school bell that her mother used to call everyone to dinner. Uh-oh. She wasn't finished. Now she wouldn't even be able to have dinner. This had been a terrible day.

The bell rang again. She heard Bradley go downstairs, taking the steps two at a time. Gloomily Sam tossed a ball of birthday wrapping paper at the basket. Missed again.

There was a rustle outside her door. A small square of paper slid on to her floor.

Dear Sam,

I officially declare a truce on the matter of your room. You may come to dinner. But under two conditions: (1) You agree to finish your room tomorrow, without fail. (2) You promise never again to let it get in such a mess.

If you accept, please sign below.

> *Love,*
> *Mum*

Sam thought about it. She took a scrap of paper from her waste-paper basket.

Dear Mum,

What are we having for dinner?

> *Love,*
> *Sam*

Dear Sam,

Macaroni and cheese, green beans, and brownies for dessert.

> *Love,*
> *Mum*

Mum:

My favourite kind with chocolate chips?

> *Sam*

Sam:

  Absolutely.

        Mum

Mum

  I accept.

        Signed,
        Samantha Slayton

Five

Dear Mr Tooth Fairy,

You aren't going to believe this, but today my tooth fell out on the front lawn. I looked all over for it, but I can't find it. I am not kidding. You can check my mouth if you want to. It's the big empty space on the upper left.

Will you give me money even though I don't have the tooth? Please?

Sincerely,
Samantha Slayton

On Sam's birthday, November fifth, she lost a tooth in the front lawn. It happened while she was running to catch the school bus. She couldn't stop to look for it. But after school she walked with her eyes to the ground until it seemed she'd inspected every blade of grey-green grass. It was no use. The tooth had disappeared.

"Where could it have gone?" Sam wondered while she was having hot chocolate to warm up.

"Maybe a bird flew by and picked it up, mistaking it for a pearl," her mother suggested, smiling to herself. Sam knew right away she was thinking about a poem. Sure enough she jumped up and scribbled something on the grocery pad.

"Maybe you swallowed it," said Bradley. He was cooking one of his mammoth after-school snacks, designed to add weight to his pathetically skinny body.

"If I swallowed it, I'd know it," Sam said positively. "What's that awful smell?"

"My pizza must be ready."

"That's a pizza?" The topping looked like grey glue with green specks.

"We didn't have any tomato sauce," Bradley explained, "so I used what was in the refrigerator. Tuna, apple sauce, onion, and green pepper, with a touch of oregano for seasoning." Ever since he'd started taking home economics in school, he thought he was a master chef. "Hey, it's good. Want a bite?"

Sam declined with a shudder. "Do you think the tooth fairy will come even though I don't have a tooth to put under my pillow?" she asked her mother.

"No way, José," said Bradley. "Cash on delivery, that's the way he runs his operation."

"I don't know his policy on lost teeth," her mother said. "You could write a note explaining the situation."

Sam nodded. Actually she wasn't too worried about the tooth fairy. She had a bigger worry on her mind. Her birthday party. She was having it on Saturday and it was a sleep-over party. The first sleep-over party she'd ever had. And she'd invited ten kids.

It had started out small. Three kids. Sam wanted Katy to come, naturally, and Rebecca. She and Rebecca appeared to be friends this year. At least they hadn't had a fight yet. But three was a bad

52

number, her mother always said. So Sam decided to invite Sara too.

When she told Rebecca on the bus, she looked disappointed. "You mean you're only inviting three kids? Everyone always has more than that. I had twelve last year."

"Well, my room's kind of small," Sam explained.

"Don't have it in your room. Have it in the family room. That way you get to watch TV all night."

"Well . . . " Sam wasn't sure her parents would like that.

"You really ought to invite Bonnie and Betsy," Rebecca went on. "They're so much fun. And they could bring makeup and do everyone's eyes."

Sam was beginning to get the feeling that Rebecca was giving this party instead of her. Still it might be fun to see what she looked like in eye makeup.

She invited Bonnie and Betsy. And then she decided to invite someone *she* liked, so she asked Heather Horowitz. Then she thought she ought to invite Meredith, since she was a friend of Heather's. And finally she decided she might as well have all the girls in her class. So she asked Susie and Victoria and Kim. Ten kids. Eleven, counting herself.

What was she actually going to *do* with ten kids for all those hours? They were too old for pin-the-tail-on-the-donkey and peanut hunts in the garden. Where would they all sleep? And what about her family? They were sure to do something embarrassing, especially her father. On Saturdays he liked to potter around the house fixing things. What if he was still wearing his weird pottering-around-the-house outfit when her guests arrived? Or he might decide to play

"Happy Birthday" on the French horn as he had last year. Or take a million pictures. Sam was afraid she'd made a terrible mistake.

Suddenly she noticed her mother staring at her.

"You seem to have drifted off somewhere. Is it your tooth?"

"No. Actually I was thinking about my party."

Her mother jumped up and got the grocery pad. "The secret of a good party is planning," she said. "So we'll need to make a few lists. Let's start with the food. I'm going to help you. Don't worry about a thing."

Sam knew she was going to worry about everything.

Her father was quite well behaved. He let Sam dress him. His French horn remained in its case. And he only took four pictures, just when she was opening her presents. After that he disappeared into his study. Her mother, too, was as close to invisible as she could be. She slipped in and out of the dining room, bringing food and taking it away, not saying a word. The only member of the family who was noticeable, it turned out, was Bradley.

"You didn't tell me you had a *brother*," Bonnie whispered to Sam.

"And he's so *cute!*" Betsy giggled.

Cute? For her party Bradley was wearing an old ripped sweatshirt which even her father, who loved old clothes, had given up on. And jeans with holes in the knees. And his brown hat which he'd worn in the rain so it had no shape. He looked like a homeless person. Bonnie and Betsy must be totally boy crazy to think that Bradley was cute.

54

Still, the party was going well so far, Sam thought. Her presents had included three stuffed animals, a makeup bag, and a heart necklace with a flower on it that Katy had painted herself. Bonnie and Betsy were the centre of attention as usual, telling stories about going to watch the seventh-grade boys play football and something hilarious that had happened in science involving a dead frog and Peter Phelps. Everyone was laughing. Especially Rebecca. She was trying hard to be their friend, Sam thought. When Betsy turned down a second slice of pizza because she was on a diet, so did Rebecca. And Sara, naturally. They also wouldn't eat any ice cream or cake. Dinner didn't take much time, as it turned out.

After that they moved into the family room to watch the video Sam had rented. Rebecca had gone with her to pick it out. It was last summer's space comedy starring Rebecca's favourite teen movie star, Matt Moon. Everyone except Katy had seen it already. But no one seemed to mind seeing it again. They all stretched out on their sleeping bags, their eyes glued to the TV screen, as Matt Moon appeared for the first time, dressed in an astronaut suit.

"Isn't he the biggest hunk you've ever seen?" Betsy sighed dreamily. "I get goose pimples just looking at him."

"Me too," breathed Rebecca.

"What about Robby Springfield?" asked Susie. "With that blond hair. And those eyes."

"He is *so* adorable," Victoria agreed. "I like him better than Matt Moon."

"Would you guys be quiet so I can hear?" Katy

protested. "Now I don't know what planet he's going to."

"It's only Mars," Bonnie told her. "This isn't the good part. Wait till he meets the Russian lady scientist on Saturn." She moved her sleeping bag closer to Betsy's, and they started whispering.

"I brought the new issue of *Teen Heart Throb*," Victoria whispered to Susie. "Want to see it?"

"Now I missed what went wrong with his retrofire rockets that made him land in the Everglades," complained Katy.

It soon became clear that no one was really going to watch the video. Bonnie and Betsy were busy whispering about boys. Susie and Victoria and Kim were busy leafing through teen magazines. Rebecca seemed torn between Matt Moon and Bonnie and Betsy. But when Eric Johnson's name was mentioned, she couldn't stand it any longer. She moved her sleeping bag next to Betsy's.

Only Katy and Sam were left watching the video.

"What planet is he on now?" asked Katy.

"Saturn, I think," said Sam.

"Saturn?" Bonnie suddenly sat up. "Hey, everyone. Watch this."

They were all quiet for about two minutes while Matt Moon kissed the Russian lady scientist during a space walk.

"Oh, wow! Can you imagine it? Weightless kissing!" Betsy rolled her eyes.

Everyone started talking at once about what weightless kissing would be like and how they'd go for a space walk with Matt Moon anytime, or even an earth walk. Katy turned up the volume on the TV.

The next thing Sam knew, Bonnie was making up Rebecca's eyes.

"Hey, you're not supposed to do that yet," Sam protested. "What if my mum comes down?"

"Why would your mum care?" said Bonnie. "My mum taught me how to put on all this stuff."

It was no use trying to explain about her mother's old-fashioned ideas, Sam thought. It was no use trying to run this party. She had the distinct feeling that it was running away from her.

Betsy did Sara's eyes and then Bonnie did Susie's. Kim and Victoria were arguing about who got to go next.

"I give up," said Katy. "I'm never going to understand this video. It's not very scientific anyway."

So Sam and Katy had their eyes done too. Bonnie said that Sam looked about fifteen. "You ought to wear eye makeup to dancing class. You've *got* to wear it next year. Everyone wears eye makeup in the seventh grade."

It was becoming clear to Sam that she was going to need a new mother for seventh grade.

Victoria spilled eye shadow on the sofa, but she assured Sam it would come out. Sam wasn't so sure. There were three huge purple polka dots on her mother's white sofa. Then Bonnie and Susie got into an argument about Robby Springfield.

"Everyone knows he dyes his hair," said Bonnie.

Susie was indignant. "His mother has the same colour hair he has. I saw them together on that comedy special Sunday night."

"Then his mother dyes her hair too."

Susie tossed a pillow at Bonnie. Bonnie threw it

back. Pillows flew through the air, and balloons, and copies of *Teen Heart Throb*. Susie and Victoria were stuffing balloons into Bonnie's sleeping bag. Rebecca was trying to stop them by popping all the balloons. It sounded like World War III had broken out in the family room.

Suddenly Sam remembered. Her mother was coming down to say good-night around eleven. She looked at the clock. It was ten fifty-seven.

"Hey, everyone. Could you quiet down for a minute?"

No one paid any attention to her.

"Sssh! My Mum's coming. Really."

Sam jumped up and ran to the light switch. She flicked off the lights just as her mother opened the door.

"Girls?" said Sam's mother. "Is everything all right?"

"Fine," said Sam quickly.

"Just fine, Mrs Slayton," said Rebecca.

Sam's mother seemed to hesitate. What if she turned on the lights and saw the eye makeup and the pillows thrown all over and the purple-spotted sofa?

"Well," she said finally, "maybe you girls ought to try to get some sleep. It's after eleven."

"That's just what we were going to do," Sam assured her. "Good night, Mum."

The door closed. There was a moment of silence.

Betsy giggled. "Now we can really have fun," she said.

It was a very long night. People kept moving their sleeping bags. And complaining that other people were crowding them. Or stepping on them. Or snoring.

That couldn't be, Sam was sure. Because no one went to sleep for hours and hours.

First they all wanted to watch TV. But they couldn't agree on which programme to watch: *The Harvey Kimmelman Show* or *The Late Movie*, which was about six wimpy college boys trying to get the campus beauty queen to notice them.

"My brother says this is a classic," Victoria told them.

"But the boys are such geeks," Bonnie objected. "Maybe Harvey will have on one of those cute English rock groups."

So they switched back and forth and argued and didn't watch anything.

After that they decided to play board games. They got out all the games in the cupboard and played each one for five minutes, and left the Monopoly money all over the floor.

Then they played a different game where you folded pieces of paper into triangles and found out who you were going to marry. Sam was going to marry Matt Moon, it turned out.

"Oh, you are so lucky!" squealed Rebecca.

Sam didn't agree. She'd been hoping for Brian Finnegan.

Then they turned on the TV again. *The Late Late Movie* was just coming on.

"Oh, wow!" said Katy. "*The Creature from the Purple Lagoon*. This one is truly a classic. My father stays up to watch it every time it's on. Wait till you see the creature in his crazy makeup."

But the creature was scary, creeping around in the mist, huge and ghostly white, devouring everything in sight.

"Why do those people keep walking around in the dark when they know the creature is out there?" Susie asked. "Why don't they call the police?"

"No one ever calls the police in movies like this," said Katy.

"Well, it's making me nervous," Susie said.

"It's making me scared to death," Heather suddenly got up and snapped off the TV.

It was unexpectedly quiet in the family room. They all looked at each other.

"What'll we do now?" asked Bonnie. "It's only one-thirty."

"I've got a great idea," said Betsy. "Let's raid the fridge."

Sam wasn't so sure that was a great idea. What would her mother say when she found her fridge empty in the morning? Also, her father was such a light sleeper, he'd probably hear them before they got near the kitchen.

Then suddenly Sam didn't care any more. She was tired of worrying all the time. This was her party and she was going to have fun.

"Hey, that's a great idea!" she said. "Come on, everyone. Follow me."

Sam led the way up the stairs. Very slowly she turned the doorknob.

The house was dark and still. The only sound Sam could hear was the grandfather clock ticking in the living room. The only light was a dim night-light in the upstairs hall.

To reach the kitchen they had to cross the front hall, then pass through the dining room. The hall was the tricky part. Some of the floorboards creaked when you stepped on them. And her parents' room was at the top of the stairs. Sam was convinced her father slept with one eye and one ear open.

Motioning Rebecca to follow her, Sam tiptoed cautiously across the hall. *Creak* went the floor.

Rebecca crossed. *Creak, creak.* Then suddenly someone hiccuped. And someone giggled.

Sam held her breath. She waited to hear her father's voice, asking what was going on.

Silence.

A minute later they were all in the dining room, stifling giggles, looking at Kim, who was trying desperately not to hiccup again.

"Hold your breath," whispered Heather.

"Swallow six times," whispered Katy.

"Ssshhh!" whispered Sam.

Kim was holding her breath and swallowing at the same time. Her cheeks bulged like a chipmunk's.

Bong, bong, struck the grandfather clock in the living room.

"Eeek!" Betsy jumped. Kim let out all her breath at once. She hiccuped loudly.

Now, thought Sam, her father would snap on the lights and come marching down the stairs. Should they stay where they were or make a run for the family room?

Nothing happened.

Sam couldn't believe it. This party must have worn him out.

She tiptoed over to the kitchen door. She could make out a dim light burning in there. Maybe her mother had left it on, expecting a raid on the fridge.

"Okay," she whispered, motioning everyone to follow her.

"Good evening, ladies."

Something was standing by the open fridge door, a cake in one hand, a bottle of milk in the other. In the dim light all they could see was wild sticking-up hair and a long flapping white gown.

"*The Creature from the Purple Lagoon*," breathed Susie.

"Eeek!"

"Help!"

"Wait," Sam began. She was going to tell them it was all right. It was only her father standing there in his weird nightshirt.

But no one was listening.

"Let me out of here!" squeaked Bonnie.

Kids were falling all over each other, backing out of the kitchen, crashing noisily into dining-room chairs, running downstairs. In a moment they were all gone.

Calmly Sam's father closed the fridge door.

"That's odd," he said. "I thought your friends came for a midnight snack."

"I guess they changed their minds," said Sam.

Her father cut himself a generous slice of birthday cake. "Have some?" he offered.

"Uh, I guess not," said Sam.

When she got downstairs, they were all in their sleeping bags. Finally everyone seemed tired out.

Sam found a sliver of unoccupied floor space between Heather and the fireplace. She turned out the light and crawled into her sleeping bag. The clock said two thirty-seven a.m.

Everything was dark and still. Sam shifted around in her sleeping bag, trying to get comfortable. She touched someone's hair.

"Sorry," she whispered.

"That's okay," Heather whispered back. "I can't go to sleep. Every time I close my eyes I see the creature."

"The Creature of the Slaytons' Kitchen," intoned Katy.

There were muffled giggles, rustlings around in sleeping bags, a pretend snore.

And then, at last, it was quiet.

When Sam woke up the next morning, she was lying in the fireplace.

* * *

Dear Kid,

This is most irregular. It is the policy of Tooth Fairy Enterprises to reimburse our customers for teeth in good condition, not for absurd rumours of teeth lost in swimming pools, toffees or front lawns. In view of your patronage in the past, however, and my inspection of your upper jaw while you were in an advanced state of slumber, I am willing to accept your story this time and allow a token payment.

Yours for smoother extractions,
T. Fairy

P.S. We are planning to excavate your front lawn for the missing tooth.

P.P.S. Are you aware that while in an advanced state of slumber, you snore? In our line of work we notice these things.

Six

Dear Journal,

This is weird. I don't know what to write.

I am starting this journal for Discover class. We can write about anything we want. No one else is supposed to look at it, ever. Who am I writing to? Myself, I guess. Miss Hoople suggested we start with a thought or a feeling or a description of something. Or we can just write words. I think I will start with words.

Here are some words I like:

orang-utan	*hug*	*aerodrome*
blimp	*toast*	*squeak*
chickadee	*soar*	*squiggle*

Here are some mean words:

bleak	*frigid*	*snarl*
jagged	*cruel*	*blade*

Here are some soft words:

fog	*pillow*	*snooze*
cuddle	*nest*	*marshmallow*

And here are a few weird words:

dandelion	*gnome*	*squeamish*
aardvark	*perambulator*	*burp*
gnu	*gargle*	*squid*

This is fun. I wonder who made up all these words. I'm going to write more about this tomorrow.

So long for now,
Sam

The letter came the week after Sam's birthday. It was from the school and was addressed to her parents.

"Very interesting," said Sam's mother as she read it.

"What's very interesting?" asked Sam.

"It seems you have been chosen to participate in the new gifted programme."

"Me?" said Sam.

She read the letter. It said that after careful testing, etc., etc., a small group of children had been selected to take part in a pilot programme for the gifted called Discover. These children would meet twice a week with a specially trained teacher, Sara Hoople, etc., etc. And sure enough there was Sam's name.

"That's really weird," said Sam.

"Sure is," agreed Bradley, taking a bite of his afternoon snack, an enormous sandwich with salami, cheese, tomatoes, onions and green peppers oozing out of the sides.

"I don't think it's weird at all," said her mother. "And I'm not a bit surprised."

"Probably it's a mistake," said Bradley. "Computer error, you know. Very common."

Sam's mother flashed him a look. He stopped talking and stuffed his onions back in his sandwich.

Secretly Sam thought Bradley was probably right. She went to the phone and called Katy.

"We got this weird letter in the mail," she began.

"We did too," said Katy.

Maybe that was it. Maybe lots of kids had got them. But it turned out only six kids in the entire sixth grade had. Marshall Tucker, the Human Encyclopedia, had got one. That was no surprise. And Greg Hopkins, the big maths brain. And Rosemary Wang. And Jessica Worthington. Sam was sorry to hear about Jessica. Since kindergarten she'd been acting as if she knew everything. It was a disappointment to find out she'd been right.

It was also a disappointment that Brian Finnegan wasn't in it. But Sam wasn't really surprised. He was gifted in sports, but not in schoolwork.

Sam was surprised about Rebecca, though. She and Sam had always got about the same grades. And Heather Horowitz. She was always studying. She couldn't go anywhere after school because she had to do her homework before dinner. Why Sam and not them?

She couldn't get used to the idea. It was too strange. She, Samantha Slayton, was *gifted*.

"This is really weird," she said to Katy.

At school everyone was talking about the gifted class. Some kids said they'd heard the gifted class was fun. You got to miss your regular classes and all you did was play games. Others said all you did was play stupid games and you had to miss your regular classes and you might even miss assemblies. "I'm glad *I'm* not in it," they said smugly.

And they looked differently at the kids who were. In a way Sam liked it. Maybe – just maybe – it wasn't true that she was the only untalented member of the Slayton family. She was smart. But in another way it was a problem. All of a sudden she was supposed to be smart every minute. In maths class when Mr Puccio asked a question, everyone seemed to be waiting for Sam or Katy to answer it. And when Sam got 100 on her spelling test, Mrs Pinkney didn't write *Good job*! up in the corner the way she used to. She seemed to *expect* Sam to get 100.

Sam didn't think she was a different person than she had been before someone decided she was gifted. But other people seemed to. Suddenly kids were calling her up to ask questions about homework. During the social-studies quiz both Jimmy Humphrey and Peter Phelps were trying to copy from her paper. And Heather wouldn't talk to her. Sam finally asked Meredith why, and she said it was just that Heather was depressed. Her father had counted on her being in the gifted class and she thought she had let him down. She didn't feel like talking to anyone.

And Brian Finnegan stole her maths homework. It happened in study hall. Sam went to get a drink of water and when she came back, her maths homework was gone. Sam glared at Jimmy Humphrey, who sat next to her. He pointed at Peter Phelps and Peter pointed at Mark Hartigan and Mark pointed at Brian Finnegan and Brian Finnegan grinned and turned bright red. Could he have done it because he liked her? Or because she was gifted? Sam was all confused.

One day she was sitting in social class and her mind was drifting. It was five minutes before the end of school. Mrs Pinkney was droning on about the Babylonians. All Sam could think about was how hungry she was. She wondered what kind of snack her mother would have for her today.

"What do you think, Sam?" asked Mrs Pinkney.

About what? wondered Sam. She hadn't heard the question.

"What factor most influenced the development of Babylonian civilisation?" Mrs Pinkney repeated.

Sam couldn't remember anything at all about Babylonian civilisation.

"Uh – the climate?" she guessed. Climate was always a likely influence on ancient civilisations.

"I'm afraid not," said Mrs Pinkney.

From the back of the room, as clearly as if she had sat right next to her, Sam heard Bonnie's voice. "Can you believe that? I thought she was supposed to be so *gifted*."

Gifted. Sam was sick of that word. She wished she had never heard of Discover class.

But that was before she met Miss Hoople.

Miss Hoople was a small, smiling, peppy person. She wore enormous round glasses that gave her the appearance of a baby owl. But what Sam noticed most was that she was excited about things. She sat in the middle of the art storeroom, the only space the school had for Discover to meet in, and she talked to them. As she talked, her eyes sparkled and her hands moved. And soon she was bustling around, handing out papers from the tall stacks that surrounded her.

"We only have an hour," she told them, "so let's get started. Which sheet would you like to tackle first?"

It turned out that Miss Hoople didn't expect

them to work by themselves, as teachers usually did. She wanted everyone to brainstorm, to think of wild ideas and not be afraid to say them out loud.

They started with a puzzle called "Can You Find the Treasure?" which had to do with an old man hiding a diamond ring in a tumbledown mansion. They were supposed to use logic to find it. Miss Hoople's excitement was catching. Soon everyone was calling out ideas. Even Greg, who seldom said anything in class. Jessica, who usually said too much, was kind of quiet. Maybe she was in shock, having discovered that she wasn't the only clever person in the world.

After they found the treasure, which was in the billiard room, they went on to a word game. Miss Hoople called it "Reinventing Language".

"Pretend you are a cave person," she said. "And you are tired of grunting and pointing to things. You think it would be handy to communicate with other cave people. So you step out of your cave and look around. Up in the sky is a large bright object. What do you think you would call it?"

"Oog," said Marshall right away.

"Good," said Miss Hoople, writing it on the blackboard.

"Glee," said Katy.

"Excellent," said Miss Hoople. "Any more?"

"Farool," said Greg.

Everyone agreed that had a royal sound, appropriate for people who might worship the sun.

They went on to name those tall things that grew up from the ground with feathery green tops.

"Fips," said Jessica.

"Typhoos," said Rosemary.

And the soft, muddy area around the cave.

"Scrog," said Sam.

"Ooshy-gooshy," said Katy.

"Ooshy-gooshy ooze," said Marshall.

When they got to naming the round thing that the cave's cleverest person had invented, which centuries later would allow Jessica's big brother to zip around in a red sports car, everyone was laughing and calling out ideas, and Miss Hoople was writing as fast as she could.

"Tor."

"Poly-poly."

"Hup."

"Maserati."

"Not fair, Marshall. No real words."

"Uh-oh, my blackboard just ran out," Miss Hoople said breathlessly. "I'm afraid we'll have to stop."

"That was fun," said Katy, her eyes bright the way they often were in Mr Speigel's class. "Can we do it again?"

"Sure," said Miss Hoople. "Maybe next time we'll compile a cave dictionary. Or maybe we'll think of our imaginary cave people in other ways. Like what else they might invent to improve their lives."

"If we invent something, could we build it?" asked Katy.

"Sure," said Miss Hoople. "We have all the supplies in the art storeroom to use."

"Oh, wow," said Katy softly.

And that was exactly how Sam felt about Discover class.

The last thing Miss Hoople did that day was hand out a composition book to each person.

"What's this for?" asked Jessica.

"This will be your journal," Miss Hoople explained. "Right now it is just a collection of blank sheets of paper. But you are going to fill it up with your ideas, drawings, inventions – anything your amazing brain comes up with. You should write in your journal every day. And maybe someday you'll look back at it and say, there it is. The first notes for my famous invention. Or my first poem. Or my first musical composition."

It sounded wild to Sam. But the thing about Miss Hoople was that she made anything seem possible. It was possible that Sam had an amazing brain. That, thought Sam, would really be something.

Dear Journal,

I am collecting more words. Today Mum and I drove to the orchard and bought apples and home-made doughnuts. Yum! When we got back, I was thinking about autumn. Here are some autumn words:

crisp	*chill*	*shrivelled*
crunchy	*golden*	*tart*
tangy	*pumpkin*	*pungent*

When I think about autumn, I see pictures in my mind. Here are some word pictures:

piles of orange pumpkins
a tart red apple
dry stalks of corn in brown fields
a carpet of crispy leaves

72

I would like to write a poem about autumn. But I can never make things rhyme. All poems don't have to rhyme though. My mother's never do. Maybe she has trouble with rhyming too.

I am going to try it. If my poem stinks, no one will ever see it.

Autumn

A leaf floats down from the sky.
Golden
Curled up
Drifting down
On a gentle breeze
To land
On a carpet of crispy leaves
Crunching beneath my feet.

Seven

Dear Katy,

You are not going to believe this. Rebecca has changed her name. From now on she wants to be called Becky. She told me on the bus. And that's not all. Sara is going to be Brett. She got it from some soap opera, Rebecca says. The reason for changing their names is they are forming a club with Bonnie and Betsy called the "Busy B's."

Isn't that stupid? They are such jerks. I can't believe I was ever friends with Rebecca.

Write back,
Sam

Sam absolutely refused to call Rebecca Becky. It sounded so dumb. Not so long ago Rebecca had thought so too. Sam remembered when they started third grade and the teacher kept calling her Becky. Rebecca corrected her every time. "No one in my family has nicknames," she said. "My father's name is Robert and my mother is Patricia and my brother is Alexander. My mother says if she'd wanted Becky and Alex, she would have named us that."

Sam had wondered then how long it could last. Kids always shortened each other's names. Sam hadn't

74

been Samantha since nursery school. But Rebecca had always insisted on being Rebecca. Until now.

Actually it didn't matter what Sam called her. She didn't see Rebecca much any more. Her mother drove her to school, so she wasn't on the bus. And in school she was always with Bonnie and Betsy and Sara (Brett). She was even beginning to look like them. She'd had her hair cut like Betsy's. She wore heart earrings. And she had Ash Can jeans. Every day the four of them came to school dressed exactly alike. Sam had a new name for them. The Bobbsey Quadruplets.

Still she had to admit she missed Rebecca. Not so much as a friend, but just talking to her on the bus. Sam hadn't realised how much information she'd picked up about clothes and boys and dancing class. She couldn't talk about any of these topics with Katy. And now something was coming up that she really needed to talk to someone about. The dancing-class Christmas party.

This was Sam's newest worry. First of all, it wasn't going to be held at the Community Centre but at a country club. Sam had never been inside a country club before. But everyone said it was very fancy and you had to be really dressed up and they served cake on real china plates and punch in little glass cups. And it was going to be like a high school dance. The boys would be asking the girls for every dance, except a few where the girls asked the boys. And parents would be there as chaperones.

The possibility of her own parents being there was too awful to contemplate. But fortunately she was at home on the afternoon the dance committee chairman called her mother. "Monday night the sixteenth?" she heard her say. Sam began shaking her head and waving her arms. "You can't," she mouthed. Her mother smiled. "I'm sorry, Mrs Farquar," she said into the phone, "but my daughter informs me I can't." When she hung up, though, her mother seemed disappointed. "I might have had the chance to dance," she said reproachfully. "If you had danced," Sam replied, "I wouldn't."

That was one less thing to worry about. But Sam still had a long list. Like what could she wear that would really be dressed up? Did stealing her homework mean Brian Finnegan liked her? Was it possible he might ask her to dance? And if by some miracle he did, would she step on his foot or trip him again? Would it be worse to dance with him and step on his foot or not to dance with him at all?

Luckily Heather was talking to her again. She seemed to have recovered from her depression about not being gifted. In maths class they spent a whole period writing notes about the Christmas party.

Dear Heather,

    I hate maths unit reviews, don't you? What are you wearing to the Christmas party? I have nothing to wear. If my mother won't buy me a dress, I can't go.

                              Write back,
                              Sam

Sam:

You have to go to the party. It's going to be fun. They give out lots of door prizes. And the food is really good, I heard.

My dress is navy with red swirly things and a white collar. I only wore it once so far, to my flute recital.

> *Write back,*
> *Heather*

Heather,

Well, I want to go but I have to get a dress. Yours sounds nice. Where did you buy it?

> *Write back,*
> *Sam*

Sam:

Farrell's pre-teen department. Third floor. I think Mr Puccio is watching us.

> *Better not write back,*
> *Heather*

Sam found something at Farrell's too. The minute she walked into the pre-teen department she saw it. The dress was pale pink with tiny blue flowers and lace on the collar and sleeves.

It fitted perfectly. And her mother liked it too. She seemed in such a good mood that Sam walked her by the rack of Ash Cans on their way out.

"*Those* are what everyone at school is wearing?" her mother exclaimed. "I can't believe it." She looked at the price tag and her mouth dropped open.

"They're on sale," Sam pointed out. "Usually they're more."

Her mother shook her head. "I've got an idea. Why don't we just take your old jeans and dip them in ashes from the fireplace?"

"Forget it," said Sam.

You couldn't win them all. At least she had a dress for the Christmas party.

On the way to the country club her father hummed. Sam cringed inside. This was why she hated to be seen with him in public. You never knew when he would do something embarrassing. One time in the supermarket checkout line he'd hummed through the entire first movement of his favourite Mozart horn concerto. Out loud. So people could hear. Sam had nudged him and glared at him, but he paid no attention. He was in a world of his own. Finally she'd switched lines.

Sam looked around to see if anyone had noticed his humming. Rebecca and Bonnie were whispering in the back seat. Jimmy Humphrey was telling a joke to Mark Hartigan. Maybe they thought it was just tyre noise. To be on the safe side Sam squeezed her father's elbow. He squeezed hers back, smiling. Sometimes he was so dense.

But driving up to the country club, Sam forgot about her father. The country club looked like a Christmas card. Candles glowed in all the windows and a Christmas tree was lit up inside the open front door. Ahead of them a line of cars pulled up, spilling out kids into the light.

"Have fun everyone," her father said.

Inside, the country club was as fancy as everyone had said. Dark wood gleamed and chandeliers glittered. Groups of elegantly dressed people glided across the soft carpet. One woman in a black dress and gold hoop earrings looked vaguely familiar to Sam. She realised with a shock that it was Sara's mother. Always before she'd seen her in jeans and a ski jacket, carrying a baby. These must be the chaperones.

Sam looked for Heather, but she didn't see her, so she followed Bonnie and Rebecca into a room called the Crystal Ballroom. From the ceiling hung a huge glass chandelier. The wallpaper was gold and so were the chairs. At one end was another Christmas tree, this one decorated entirely with gold angels.

Sam felt strange in this room. Everything looked fragile. And the dark polished floor felt slippery, like ice. But then she noticed all the girls gathered along one wall, talking as usual. And all the boys along the other wall, fooling around as usual. There was Brian Finnegan, looking cute in his grey suit and a bright red tie. Chubby Cheeks was in his same old beige outfit. And Mr Dunphy was adjusting the music system. The Christmas party was beginning to look like dancing class.

"Hi," said a voice behind her. It was Heather.

Sam was glad to see her. "I like your dress," she said.

"I like yours too," said Heather. "I told you Farrell's was good."

"Good evening, everyone," said Mr Dunphy in his cheery voice. "And welcome to our annual Christmas party."

79

As it turned out, the Christmas party was exactly like dancing class. The boys stampeded across the floor, trying to beat each other to the same few girls. Sam was not one of them. Neither was Heather. When the rushing around was over, both of them were still sitting in the chairs.

And Brian Finnegan was dancing with Bonnie. He hadn't even looked at Sam. Stealing her homework hadn't meant a thing.

It was kind of awful sitting in the chairs while everyone else was dancing. There was nothing to do and nowhere to hide. Sam counted how many girls were wearing red or green dresses. She tried to decide which boys were the worst dancers. Jimmy Humphrey was probably the worst, but Brian Finnegan was up there in the top five. And she studied Betsy, dancing with Eric Johnson, trying to figure out her secret. Of course, she was cute, with her blue eyes and blonde hair. And she had a way of smiling up at the boy she was dancing with. That was because she was so short. She also seemed to be able to talk while she danced, without falling down. Why hadn't Sam been born cute and short and able to dance and talk at the same time?

Chubby Cheeks asked Sam for the second dance. For a minute she was glad. Anything had to be better than sitting in the chairs. But actually it wasn't. Chubby Cheeks talked the entire time about his model-aeroplane collection. His conversation was so boring, Sam thought, it should be recorded on tape for people who had trouble falling asleep. Two minutes of Chubby Cheeks and they'd drop right off.

After that was ladies' choice.

"Here's what we have to do," Heather whispered. "Pick out a cute boy and be fast and pushy. And if you can, trip Bonnie or Betsy on your way across the floor."

A cute boy. Brian Finnegan. Sam's heart was suddenly pounding in her ears. But no, she couldn't ask him. He didn't like her. And he would know she liked him. That would be terrible.

"Come on," urged Heather. "You don't want to sit in the chairs again, do you?"

Sam decided to ask the tall boy with glasses. At least she'd be dancing with someone her own size.

"Young ladies, you may invite a gentleman to dance," announced Mr Dunphy.

Sam felt the way she did at the start of the fifty-yard dash. Ready, set, go! And she was off across the floor, aiming at the tall boy with glasses. But Rebecca darted in front of her – probably on her way to capture Eric Johnson – and a tiny dark-haired girl beat Sam to him. Not fair. She ought to stick to boys her own size. Sam looked around for someone else. Chubby Cheeks? She couldn't bear it again. Jimmy Humphrey? She'd be risking her toes, but at least she knew him.

Sam made a dash for Jimmy. So did another girl in a blue dress.

"Would you care to . . . " began Sam.

The other girl elbowed past her.

" . . . dance?"

Somehow Jimmy Humphrey was gone, swept on to the dance floor. And instead Sam was face to face with Brian Finnegan.

"If we have to, we have to," he said glumly.

He didn't want to dance with her. Well, she hadn't meant to ask him. It was a mistake. But she couldn't take it back now. Sam could feel her face turning pink.

"Dancing has got to be the dumbest thing ever invented," he complained. They were on the dance floor now, and Brian was the one who was stepping on her feet and he wasn't even saying he was sorry. "You walk around in circles, going no place, to some terrible music. What's the point?"

Sam couldn't answer. She felt a little better though. It wasn't that Brian didn't want to dance with her. He didn't want to dance at all.

"I wasn't going to come tonight," he went on. "I told my mother I was sick. But she shoved a thermometer in my mouth. Then she got my two older brothers to dress me and throw me in the car, and drive me over. I couldn't escape."

"Oh," said Sam. "Well, the food is supposed to be good. And they give lots of door prizes."

Brian brightened a little. "I heard there are gift certificates to Sam's Music Store and the Sports Corner. Hey, what number have you got?"

Sam took her door-prize ticket out of her glove. "Eighty-eight."

"*Eighty-eight?*" He stopped in the middle of the dance floor. "Eight is my lucky number! You've got to swop with me."

Sam wasn't sure it was allowed. But she couldn't say no to Brian Finnegan.

"Okay," she said.

They swopped tickets and danced some more. Sam

was in a state of shock. She couldn't believe that she and Brian Finnegan were actually dancing.

Then the music ended. Mr Dunphy announced it was time for refreshments, and Brian bounded off, grinning, to be first in line.

Sam got in line with Heather.

"I saw you dancing with Brian Finnegan," she said. "Poor you. Are you crippled for life?"

Sam felt her face turning pink again.

"Oh, no. Don't tell me you really *like* him!" Heather whispered.

"Ssshh!" Mark Hartigan and Peter Phelps were right in front of them. And the Bobbsey Quadruplets in their matching red and white dresses were in front of them. "I'll tell you later," Sam whispered back.

The refreshment line moved slowly. Sam watched the tall white cake with peppermint icing shrink, and the level of pink punch gradually grow lower. Finally they were almost there. Rebecca was filling her punch cup.

Eric Johnson suddenly appeared from nowhere, stepping into line in front of Heather.

She tapped him on the shoulder. "What do you think you're doing?"

"Getting in line with my friend Mark." Eric grinned his adorable grin.

"Pushing in, you mean," said Heather.

"You could say that," admitted Eric.

"Well, you can't do it." Heather stepped in front of him.

"Oh, no?" Eric stepped in front of her.

"No!"

Heather gave him an elbow. Eric bumped into

the back of his friend Mark. Mark bumped into Peter Phelps, who bumped into Rebecca. Rebecca's punch cup fell to the floor with a crash.

"Oh, my dress!" squealed Betsy.

In the middle of her white skirt was a large bright pink circle.

"I'm sorry," said Rebecca. She looked down. "My gloves!" Her white gloves had turned suddenly pink.

Two of the refreshment ladies were dabbing at Betsy's dress with napkins. But the spot wasn't coming out. It seemed to be getting darker. "What am I going to do?" wailed Betsy.

Finally the refreshment ladies took Rebecca and Betsy off to the ladies' room to try to wash out the spots.

Sam and Heather looked at each other.

"Do you think it will come out?" asked Sam.

"Pink punch never comes out," said Heather.

They grinned at each other.

"Actually," said Heather, "this party isn't turning out to be so bad."

The rest of the party wasn't bad at all. Sam and Heather sat in the chairs and whispered and watched the door for Rebecca and Betsy. Finally they came back. Rebecca's hands were behind her back. Sam couldn't tell if there was still a pink circle on Betsy's skirt, but her dress looked kind of limp. In fact Rebecca and Betsy looked limp.

On the next ladies' choice Sam was fast and pushy and got to dance with the tall boy with glasses. His name was Jeff, she found out. It was refreshing to look at a boy's navy-blue shoulder while dancing instead of down at the top of his head. Then she danced with Chubby Cheeks again. And a pale skinny boy with big front teeth who reminded her of a chipmunk.

"Do you like Russell?" he asked.

"Who's Russell?"

"Russell Farquar. You know." He jerked his head to the side. There was Chubby Cheeks, looking at her.

"Him?" said Sam. "No, I hate him."

"Oh," said the chipmunk boy.

He didn't say another word for the rest of the dance.

When she got back to the chairs. Sam told Heather about the chipmunk boy and Chubby Cheeks.

"It's kind of nice to have *someone* like you," Heather said wistfully.

Sam thought about it. It was true, she decided. It was kind of nice. Even if it was only old Chubby Cheeks.

And then the music system was playing "White Christmas", and Mr Dunphy was picking the winners of the six door prizes out of a red stocking cap.

"Number forty-two," he called. "Eighteen. Sixty-four. Ten. Thirty-one. Seventy-nine."

Thirty-one. Sam looked at the ticket stub in her hand in surprise. "That's me!"

Out of the corner of her eye she saw Brian Finnegan scowling as she walked up to receive her prize. It was a ten-dollar gift certificate to Sam's Music Store.

"Oh, you are so lucky!" said Heather.

All in all, Sam was inclined to agree.

Dear Sam,

What happened at the Christmas party anyway? The Busy B's have been buzzing about it all morning. Betsy is mad at her mother because she said she won't buy her any more clothes for the rest of the year. And Bonnie is mad at Becky because it was all her fault. And Brett is mad at Bonnie for being mad at Becky.

This sounds good. I almost wish I'd been there.

Write back,
Katy

Dear Katy,

Meet me at the baby swings at recess and I'll tell you all about it.

Sam

Eight

Dear Journal,

I am writing to you because Miss Hoople says when you are upset, it is good to write down your thoughts. It helps sort out your feelings.

I just found out that my mother is thinking about running away from home. She always jokes about it, but I never thought she was serious. My mother is dissatisfied with her life. She thinks she got married too young. She would like to have had a career as a poet, but her family has stood in her way. She didn't exactly say it, but probably she wishes she'd never had children.

I am really worried. Should I tell her I know? Should I tell my father? Or Bradley? Or should I just keep quiet and let her make her own decision?

The trouble with writing to you is you can't answer my questions. But writing down my thoughts has helped sort out one of my feelings. I am not going to tell Bradley. He would just laugh and call me a dim-witted fool. This is his latest put-down. I will write more tomorrow.

Wish you could write back,
Sam

Sam first found out about her mother on a gloomy day in January. It was a snow day, the first of the season. All morning she had been reading, and she had finished all her library books. She had talked on the phone to Katy and Heather. And she'd written three letters. What else was there to do?

Looking out of her window, Sam checked on the snow. There must be about ten inches now. If it were last year, she and Bradley would be sledding. But this year Bradley saw snow only as a way to make money. He was out shovelling driveways. If Sam were still friends with Rebecca she could go sledding on her hill. But she had a feeling Rebecca didn't go sledding any more. She probably thought it was too babyish.

She looked around her room for something else to read. There was always *Little Women*. But she'd just read it for the fourth time during Christmas vacation. Her eye fell on a stack of magazines. Because of her writing, her mother subscribed to lots of them. Sometimes if Sam was desperately bored, she would look through them.

Sam picked up the magazine on top. It was *Today's Woman*, with a picture of Bobbi Sue Morgan on the cover. Inside, it said, you could learn how Bobbi Sue successfully combined her careers as country music singer, movie star, wife of a prominent business executive, and mother of four. Sam was always interested in how people managed this, since it seemed so hard to be just one of those things.

She leafed through the magazine. Along the way she noticed another article, entitled "How Satisfied Are You with Your Life?" You were supposed to fill in a questionnaire and send it in. With the help of their readers, the editors of *Today's Woman* said they hoped to learn how American women felt about their lives today.

Sam was delighted to help. She loved to fill in questionnaires. She got a pencil and stretched out on her bed.

The first group of questions had the heading: "Tell Us about Yourself." And the first question was "How old are you?" As Sam was about to write her age, she saw that the space was already filled in: "39".

She glanced down the page. All the spaces were filled in. Her mother must have answered the questionnaire and then forgotten to send it in.

This was kind of disappointing. Sam started to turn to the Bobbi Sue Morgan article. But then she felt a flicker of curiosity. Was her mother satisfied with her life?

The first group of questions didn't tell her anything she didn't already know. Her mother's age, race, religion, education, marital status. She was a little surprised that her mother listed her occupation as "Homemaker". She'd have thought she would call herself a writer.

Next was "Tell Us about Your Family". Bradley and Sam were mentioned, and her mother's two sisters, and whether anyone in the family was divorced or not. Then came the question "If you had it to do over again, would you have the same size family?" The possible answers were: "Same. More Children. Fewer Children. No Children. Not sure." There was a black pencil dot next to "No children", as if her mother had started to mark it. And a tick next to "not sure". What did that mean? Sam couldn't figure it out, but it made her nervous.

After that came "Tell Us about Your Career". Her mother's answers to these questions were surprising. Sam hadn't known she had been a prize-winning poet in college. Or that her ambition had been to win the Nobel Prize for Literature. Then she came to two questions that made her catch her breath. "Do you feel you have fulfilled your career ambitions?" Her mother had ticked "No." "If not, what do you feel has stood in your way?" And her mother had ticked "Family responsibilities."

Sam was beginning to feel extremely odd. It was as if she had accidentally stumbled on her mother's private journal. She felt guilty about reading her secrets. She didn't even want to know all these things about her mother. And yet she had to keep reading.

She especially did not want to know the answers to the next group of questions. "Tell Us about Your Love Life". They started off all right. "How long have you been married?" "When you met, was it love at first sight?" ("No," said her mother.) But then they started asking questions like "Are you satisfied with your sex life?" ("Yes," said her mother.) Sam felt embarrassed, even though she was alone in her room. Fortunately they didn't go into the details. And then "What about your husband would you most like to change?" Instead of "Nothing", her mother had ticked "He works too hard". And: "When you go out, do you ever look at other men?" ("Yes," said her mother.) And: "What do you notice first about a man?" ("His body," said her mother.)

His *body*? Sam couldn't believe it. What was

wrong with her mother? She was nearly forty years old, for heaven's sake. And a married woman.

But maybe she wished she weren't. Because the next question was "Have you ever had any regrets about your marriage?" And her mother had ticked "Married too young". That was followed by "If you had your life to live over, what would you change?" "Would pursue a career first," answered her mother.

Sam was really getting concerned now. It appeared that her mother was dissatisfied with everything in her life. How long had this been going on? Did her father know? No wonder her mother seemed quiet lately. She was depressed. She wished she were living alone in a little cottage somewhere, writing poetry.

And then Sam came to the final question. "Have you ever thought of giving up everything and running away?"

Very firmly in dark black pencil her mother had ticked "Yes".

For several days Sam brooded about what to do. She studied her father for signs of concern. But he was in the midst of one of his mathematical breakthroughs. He didn't hear when you spoke to him. When he took out the rubbish, he didn't come back, and Bradley reported that he was wandering around the patio with a black plastic rubbish bag under his arm. And in the middle of the night he paced the house, talking to himself. It was quite possible, Sam thought, that he had no idea what was going on in her mother's life.

She studied her mother for signs of depression. She had read another article called "The Seven Signs of

Depression: How to Tell If You Need Help". Sam thought she recognised two of them in her mother. She definitely looked tired. But that could be due to Sam's father waking her up at night with his pacing. And at meals she only picked at her food. This might be due to lack of appetite, as the article said, or it might be just that she'd gone on another one of her diets.

By the end of the week Sam couldn't stand it any more. This was a crisis. She had to talk to someone. Her father seemed like the best choice. It was his wife, after all, who was about to run away. If anyone could stop her, he could.

But she had to get him alone, when he wasn't thinking deep mathematical thoughts. He was always asking her to go jogging with him. Maybe that would be a good time.

On Saturday morning her father disappeared into his study. Three hours later he emerged, blinking, with that what-planet-am-I-on? look on his face.

"Anyone want to go jogging?" he asked.

"I will," Sam volunteered.

Her father looked surprised. "Great," he said. "I'll change and be ready in five minutes."

When she saw him, Sam nearly changed her mind. He was wearing one of his typical weird outfits: a turtleneck with stretched-out collar, a grey sweatshirt that she knew for a fact he'd had since high school, and droopy green tracksuit trousers. For Christmas Sam's mother had bought him a navy-blue running suit. He had said it was beautiful, but he never wore it. It was too nice.

It would be embarrassing to be seen with him. But Sam had to do it. This was important.

She thought she'd better start talking before she lost her courage. "Uh – Dad," she began.

But her father wasn't listening. He was doing something peculiar with his arms, swinging them in circles, like a windmill. "Stretch those muscles, Sam," he urged.

She'd forgotten. He always insisted on warm-up exercises before jogging.

Now her father was swinging his left leg, as if trying to get rid of a swarm of attacking mosquitoes. And then his right leg. Sam glanced around to see if the people next door were watching.

"Well, I'm all loosened up. How about you?"

Sam nodded.

"Then let's go."

They jogged easily down the road.

"Isn't this great?" said Sam's father, smiling at her.

Sam smiled back. He had an odd way of running, she noticed, with his feet turned in, like a duck. Probably all the neighbours were watching out of their windows, laughing.

They reached the end of the block and started back. Another thing about her father, he didn't run very fast. She had enough breath left over to talk.

How should she bring up the topic of her mother? *Did you know Mum is thinking of leaving you*? No. Too cruel.

How about something casual like *Dad, I was wondering. What is your opinion about combining marriage and a career*? No. Too subtle. And she didn't want to get into the problems of modern society. This was the kind of topic her father could discuss for hours.

Either she was speeding up or her father was slowing down. Sam forced herself to run slower so they could jog next to each other. But then he slowed down even more. What was the matter with him?

Sam glanced back. Uh-oh. She could tell by her father's eyes that he was going into a maths trance.

"Dad," she blurted out, "I think Mum wants to go away."

He blinked. Finally his eyes focused on her. "I know," he said glumly.

This was even more of a crisis than she'd realised. Her mother and father must have discussed it. Was her mother leaving soon? Was it possible they were getting a divorce.

"She wants to go to Buffalo."

"Buffalo?" Sam thought runaway wives usually went to California or Paris. Or some warm island somewhere.

"To visit Aunt Betty for Easter. I don't know if I can finish the problem I'm working on. But if I can, we'll go for the long weekend."

Sam couldn't believe her ears. She was talking about the breakup of her family, and her father was talking about a long weekend in Buffalo. Somewhere along the way there had been a major misunderstanding.

Then she saw her mother coming down the driveway in her pale-pink running suit. She waved. A minute later she was jogging next to them.

"Hey, slowcoach." She poked Sam's father in the ribs. "Move those buns. This is supposed to be aerobic for the body, not the brain."

Her mother and father grinned at each other.

And her father actually moved his buns a little faster.

Sam was thoroughly confused. What was going on here, anyway?

The three of them sat at the kitchen table, sipping hot chocolate. Sam loved sitting around the round oak table with a fire going in the wood-burning stove, watching her marshmallow melt into a plump white island in the middle of her cocoa. It made her feel cosy inside.

Her mother seemed to feel that way too. She smiled at Sam and Sam's father. "This is one of those moments that make it all worthwhile. I guess I won't run away from home this week."

Sam's insides turned suddenly cold. This was her chance. Taking a deep breath she said, "Mum, would you ever really run away from home?"

Her mother seemed startled. "Oh, my. I guess I do say that a lot. I'm sorry, Sam. Sometimes I feel frustrated, but no, I would never really run away. I couldn't leave you or Bradley or Mr Maths Whiz here. You're my family."

"But . . . " Sam hesitated. Then she decided she might as well say it all. "If you hadn't got married so young and had children, you could have had a career. You could have been a famous poet."

For a minute Sam wondered if she'd said too much. Her mother was staring as if she could see inside her head.

"Maybe I could have been a better poet if I'd worked on it harder," she said thoughtfully. "Or maybe I just like to think so. But I made my own choices. I met this boy with wild hair who wanted to discuss temperature inversions on my very first day of college. I had to marry him so he wouldn't get hit by a car while he was lost in the mathematical clouds. And I wanted very much to have children. It turns out you can't have everything, that's all."

"Once I wanted to be a French-horn player," her father added softly. "I thought I would love to play music all day long. But I also loved to solve maths problems. I had to choose. Now I'll never know if I could have played the French horn in the New York Philharmonic."

Sam hadn't realised life was so complicated for adults too. If her parents had made different choices, she might have had a Nobel Prize-winning poet for a mother and a famous musician for a father. But then, of course, they might never have met each other. And she would never have been born.

"So there you have it, Sam," her mother said. "Nothing is perfect. We always seem to want more than we can have. But most days I'm happy with my life."

"Except the days when you're not," said her father.

Sam's mother smiled. "Well, you know you could have waited a few years before sweeping me off my feet with your smooth talk about temperature inversions."

"If I'd waited a few years, I might not have been so pathetic-looking and you wouldn't have had that overwhelming urge to take care of me."

Her parents were laughing now. The fire popped in the stove. The kitchen felt cosy again.

Sam saw that her marshmallow had melted to

just the right consistency. She picked it up with her spoon. It slid down her throat, fat and slimy and warm.

Dear Journal,

Well, my mother isn't planning to run away from home after all. Sometimes she feels like it, but she would never really do it. That is because she couldn't be without her family. I think she is glad she has children. I know I am.

We are definitely going to Buffalo for Easter. Probably it will snow the entire time we are there, even though it will be in April. I have sorted out my feelings about Buffalo. I hate it. But I have to go.

So long for now,
Sam

Nine

Dear Mr Tooth Fairy,

Here is another tooth that I got pulled out today. It is a perfect tooth – no cavities! I didn't lose it on the front lawn. Plus I went through extreme suffering for you. So I think I deserve a bonus. How about seventy-five cents this time?

Sincerely yours,
Samantha Slayton

P.S. My mum said I was extremely brave.

Sam had a job. Her first baby-sitting job. Mrs Mattingly from across the street had asked Bradley to baby-sit, but he was going to a basketball game, so then she asked Sam. They weren't going to be out late. And there was only one boy to take care of, a seven-year-old named Christopher. "Please, please, please!" Sam had begged. And her mother had said yes.

She was a little nervous about it. She wasn't quite sure how a baby-sitter was supposed to act. Should she try to appear really grown-up and strict to make sure the boy did what she said? Or would it be better just to try to be friends with him?

Bradley said you had to be tough. "Otherwise

they'll walk all over you," he told her. "They'll throw stuff around and eat up all the sweets in the house and refuse to go to bed. You *have* to get them to go to bed. Baby-sitting is easy money if the kids are asleep. Otherwise it's a pain in the neck." Bradley ought to know. He had even baby-sat for the Mitchell boys, whom everyone called the "Two Terrors".

Talking to Bradley made Sam even more nervous. It suddenly came back to her how she and Bradley used to act when they had a baby-sitter. They would get out all the games and spread the pieces around and then let the baby-sitter clean up. And after they went to bed, they never went to sleep. Bradley would sneak into her room and they'd have pillow fights. Sam wondered if baby-sitters had referred to her and Bradley as the "Two Terrors".

She called Katy to discuss it. Katy had been taking care of the three-year-old girl next door. She seemed to like baby-sitting.

"Emily is so cute," she said. "We dress up her dolls and dance to records on the record player and read books."

"Does she go to bed when you tell her?" Sam asked.

"Sometimes she tells *me* it's bedtime. She is so good."

Baby-sitting with the Mitchell boys and with Emily sounded like two totally different experiences. Sam wondered what Christopher would be like. She decided to start out trying to be friends with him. If that didn't work, she could always get tough.

* * *

"Come in, Samantha," said Mrs Mattingly, smiling at her. "Christopher is in the kitchen. I was just getting dinner ready for the two of you."

Christopher was sitting at the table in his dressing-gown. He looked neat and clean. The kitchen looked neat and clean. Sam could tell this was the way Mrs Mattingly kept things. She relaxed a little. Maybe this job would be easy.

"Now I'll just take the pizza out of the microwave and everything will be ready," said Mrs Mattingly.

"Can I help?" asked Sam.

"No, you just sit and keep Christopher company."

Sam sat down. She felt like a guest. She glanced over at Christopher. But he was looking down at his salad.

Mrs Mattingly served the pizza. It was pepperoni, Sam's favourite. "Let's see," she said. "There's ice cream in the freezer for dessert. Don't bother about the dishes. I'll do them later. Christopher's bed-time is eight-thirty. No TV for him tonight, but there are lots of games to play and books to read. Oh, here's the number of the restaurant where we'll be in case of emergency. Do you have any questions?"

Sam couldn't think of any.

"Oh, I almost forgot. There's Lucy."

A chubby tan cocker spaniel wandered into the room.

"Lucy has had her dinner. You don't need to worry about her. You won't even know she's here."

Lucy lay down under the table with a little sigh.

"Well, Daddy is waiting. Good night, Christopher. We'll be back no later than ten."

She kissed Christopher and hurried out of the door.

The kitchen was suddenly quiet. Sam smiled at Christopher. But he was still staring into his salad bowl. Was there a bug in his lettuce? She tried to think of something friendly to say. Her brain seemed empty. What did seven-year-old boys like to talk about anyway?

Sam chewed on her pizza. Christopher chewed on his pizza.

She could ask him what he liked to do. No, that sounded dumb. What grade was he in? She knew what grade he was in. What did he want to be when he grew up? Yuck. That was what old lady friends of your parents always asked.

Now Sam had finished her pizza. And still neither of them had said a single word.

"Want some ice cream?" she asked abruptly.

Christopher nodded.

It wasn't exactly a conversation, but it was something. She got up to get the ice cream. A low growl came from under the table. What was wrong with Lucy? Sam wasn't supposed to know she was there. Well, maybe it had just been a snore.

Sam dished out the ice cream and sat down again. Why didn't Christopher say anything? Maybe he didn't like her. Maybe he had really wanted Bradley for his baby-sitter and was mad that he'd got his sister instead.

She couldn't stand being at this silent table any longer. She ate her ice cream so fast her teeth hurt. As she stood up, she heard another sound from under the table. This time she was sure of it.

Lucy was growling at her. Great. The dog didn't like her either.

Mrs Mattingly had said not to bother with the dishes. But she ought to at least scrape them. Sam looked for the rubbish bin. She didn't see one.

"Where does the rubbish go?" she asked.

"Under the sink," said Christopher.

She had said something and he had answered. It was a real conversation.

"Thanks," said Sam.

But he didn't say, "You're welcome." Instead he left the room. Sam took out the rubbish bin. She scraped the dishes and put them in the sink. What else should she do? Oh, yes, wipe the table.

But when she approached the table, Lucy growled at her again. "Nice dog," Sam said soothingly. But Lucy growled louder. Sam gave up. There was only a little salad dressing and a few pieces of pepperoni on the table anyway.

She went to find Christopher. He was lying on the sofa in the family room, reading.

"Good book?" she asked.

"Kind of."

"What's it about?"

"Space."

"You mean, like rockets and orbiting space stations?"

"Just regular space."

"Oh."

Silence.

Sam had never realised what hard work it was to keep a conversation going. She forced herself to keep trying.

"Do you want to play games, like your mum said?"

"I don't care."

"What have you got?"

Christopher pulled out a pile of games from a cupboard.

"Oh, Mastermind, my favourite. Want to play that?"

"Okay."

Sam was good at Mastermind. They played two games and she won them both. Christopher didn't appear to be having much fun. All through the two games he didn't say a word. Maybe he felt bad about losing.

"Now you pick a game," she suggested.

He chose Battleship. This time Sam let him win. But that didn't seem to perk him up. Maybe he didn't like games. Or maybe he was just extremely shy. Sam sneaked a glance at the clock. Only seven forty-five. Time was really creeping along. What could they possibly do for forty-five minutes until his bedtime?

"What would you like to do now?" she asked.

Christopher shrugged. "We could play with the computer."

"Is it okay with your mum?"

"Sure."

For a seven-year-old Christopher knew a lot about computers. He slipped in a disk and complicated designs appeared on the screen. He slipped in another disk and drew a complicated design himself. "You can do that," he said. "I'll show you how."

Suddenly Christopher was talking. He showed her a programme he was writing. And a game about finding a buried treasure. It was a hard game. Sam kept falling over a cliff and dying. But Christopher got all the way to the cave where a masked man armed with a rifle, an axe and a bow-and-arrow stood guard over the treasure.

Before Sam knew it the clock had sped to eight-thirty.

"Hey, Christopher," she said, "it's your bedtime."

"Just fifteen more minutes," he begged. "Please?"

Sam hesitated. Now was the time to be tough. If she let him stay up fifteen more minutes, probably he'd never go to bed. He would walk all over her, just as Bradley had said.

"Okay," she agreed.

At eight forty-five Christopher turned off the computer and went upstairs to bed. Sam breathed a sigh of relief.

"Do you need anything?" she asked.

"No."

"Well, good night."

"Good night."

All in all this baby-sitting job had been easy. Except for the conversation. Still, a shy kid was definitely better than a terror. Now came the best part, as Bradley had said. All she had to do was watch TV until his parents came home.

Sam made herself comfortable on the sofa. She was a little hungry. But if she went to the kitchen, she might get growled at by Lucy. Better stay away from the dog. She picked up the remote control and flicked around the channels. Good, her favourite nine o'clock comedy show was on.

The girls at Miss Higgins's Country Day School had just tricked the headmistress into dying her hair purple when Lucy ambled into the room. Sam looked up, surprised. She was even more surprised when Lucy jumped up on the sofa. Had she suddenly decided to be friends?

It seemed that way. Lucy curled up next to her, her head resting on Sam's knee. This sudden affection made Sam nervous. Maybe it was a trick. Maybe Lucy was secretly planning to bite her. Or maybe it was just that Sam was sitting in her favourite sleeping place.

That must be it. Very carefully Sam stood up and moved over to the armchair. Lucy seemed to think it over for a minute. Then she moved to the armchair too.

Sam got up and went back to the sofa. Lucy followed. What was going on here anyway?

Lucy whined, looking up at Sam with mournful brown eyes. And then, suddenly, she threw up all over the sofa.

Sam leaped up. Oh, no! The dog was sick, that was why she was so friendly. Disgusting! Her baby-sitting consultations hadn't prepared her for this. What did she do now?

Sam looked down at her jeans. Well, at least she hadn't got anything on her. She looked at Lucy. What if she was going to be sick again? Sam had better get her out of the family room before she ruined the rug. But how? She couldn't stand to touch her.

Strangely enough, Lucy seemed okay now. She wagged her tail in an apologetic way and retreated to the kitchen. Sam looked at the sofa. The sofa was not okay. The middle cushion was a disgusting mess.

It occurred to Sam that this was an emergency.

She'd better call Mr and Mrs Mattingly at the restaurant and tell them to come home.

She turned off the TV and went to find the phone number. In the kitchen the rubbish bin was tipped over. Soggy lettuce, eggshells, and scrunched-up napkins were strewn over the floor. That was why Lucy was sick. She had eaten the rubbish.

Sam paused with the phone in her hand. Maybe she shouldn't call. It wasn't a true emergency. Actually it was Sam's fault this had happened. She had left the rubbish out. She ought to clean up the mess.

How would her mother do it? Sam remembered the time when Bradley was eight and he'd stood in the upstairs hall saying, "I think I'm going to be sick. I think I'm going to be sick." And he had been sick, before he could make it to the bathroom. Water, Sam thought. Plenty of water.

Holding her breath and trying not to look, Sam carried the sofa cushion to the kitchen. She mopped it with dry paper towels. Then she scrubbed it with wet paper towels. She used up almost a whole roll. The smell was terrible. Sam thought she might be sick herself.

Finally the pillow looked pretty good. She glanced at the clock. Nine-forty. Mr and Mrs Mattingly might be back any minute. If they found the house in a huge mess, they'd never ask her to baby-sit again.

Sam hurried to the family room. She dropped the cushion on the sofa, scooped up the games, and shoved them into the cupboard. Then she dashed back to the kitchen to clean up the floor.

Lucy watched her from under the table.

"You know what you are?" Sam said. "A trouble-maker, that's what."

Lucy wagged her tail. It appeared they were friends now.

Sam wiped the table, put the rubbish bin under the sink, and ran back to the family room. Oops, she'd missed a couple of battleships under the coffee table. Sam threw them in the cupboard. Then she straightened the sofa cushions.

She had just sat down in the armchair and turned on the TV when she heard a key in the front door.

"Hi, Samantha," said Mrs Mattingly. "We had such a lovely evening. My, things look nice and peaceful here. Did everything go all right?"

"Uh – just fine," said Sam.

"It was awful," Sam told her parents.

"You poor kid," said her mother.

"Sounds a little more exciting than you expected," said her father.

"The dog got sick?" Bradley walked in with his bedtime snack of four scoops of ice cream. "That's nothing. One time when I was baby-sitting for the Mitchells, one kid jumped off the top bunk and got a major bloody nose and while I was cleaning him up, the other kid flushed all his baseball cards down the toilet. I had to get the next-door neighbours to call a plumber."

"And what about the time your friend Josh set off the Wrigleys' burglar alarm and three police cars surrounded the house?" Sam's father remembered.

Everyone was smiling. Even Sam. Baby-sitting seemed to be an exciting business.

"Do you know what I think is significant about this whole unfortunate incident?" her mother said.

"What?" asked Sam.

"You didn't call us. You figured out what had to be done and you went ahead and did it yourself."

Sam had never even thought of calling her parents. She'd been so busy, it hadn't popped into her mind.

"Yes," agreed her father. "That is significant."

He reached out and pulled Sam into his lap. She didn't really fit any more. Her legs stuck out and bumped into the coffee table.

Her mother smiled at her. "Sam," she said, "you are growing in all directions."

Dear Kid,

Good grief? How many departing teeth do you have, anyway? I think I and my organisation deserve a break. Winter is a busy season for us, you know. We get a lot of front teeth from the ice-skating crowd.

Well, I guess the superb condition of the specimen and the extreme suffering you describe do qualify you for a bonus. But remember, no more extractions for at least a week. I need my beauty sleep.

Yours for cool gums,
T. Fairy

Ten

Dear Sam,

I hate it when you won't talk to me. Will you at least write back and tell me why you are angry? Please write back.

Love,
Mum

Dear Mum,

I can't tell you now. Maybe later.

Sam

Sam first noticed it at her soccer game. She played full-back and there was nothing to do when the ball was at the other end of the field. She happened to look over at the sidelines where all the mothers were standing. Something about her mother was different, Sam noticed. She was wearing a hat.

How embarrassing. None of the other mothers wore hats. Sam spoke to her about it on the way home.

"Why did you have to wear a hat at the game?"

Her mother looked surprised. "To keep my head warm, of course."

"That hat is weird."

It was a striped ski hat, the kind little kids wore. It even had a pom-pom on top.

Her mother smiled. "Well, maybe you can help me pick out a better one."

"All hats are weird," Sam muttered.

"I see." Sam's mother glanced at her thoughtfully. "Is there anything else about me that bothers you?"

Now that she mentioned it, there were a few things. Sam had always known her father was a little strange, but it was only recently that she'd begun to notice her mother's peculiarities. Her jacket, for example. It was a faded, frayed survival jacket from L. L. Bean, stuffed with something puffy that made her mother resemble a hotdog in a bun. None of the other mothers had jackets like that. Her mother loved it. She said it was warm and she intended to wear it for ever. Then there was her hair. It was beginning to turn grey around the edges. None of the other sixth-grade mothers had grey hair. And her mother didn't wear makeup. Sometimes she even forgot to put on lipstick. And her laugh was too loud.

Sam didn't know which of these things to mention. She didn't want to hurt her mother's feelings.

"Well," she said finally, "could you maybe buy a new jacket?"

"I could," said her mother, "but I don't want to. I'm beginning to get the idea that you would like me to look like Bonnie's mother."

Actually her mother had read Sam's mind. Bonnie had the perfect mother. She always looked as if she had just come from the beauty salon. Her hair was perfectly styled, she wore lots of makeup, and her clothes were the latest fashion. She even had Ash

110

Can jeans. Bonnie said her mother's favourite thing to do was go shopping with her. They were like sisters, she said.

Sam's mother shook her head regretfully. "I'd like to please you, Sam, but I don't think I can do it. All that shopping and manicuring takes time. I wouldn't get any writing done. And I never did learn to put on makeup right." The thought of her mother wearing eye shadow did seem a little silly.

"You don't need to look like Bonnie's mother," Sam reassured her. "Really. But could you just try to act like a regular mother?"

"I'm not sure I know what that means," said her mother. "But I'll give it a try. From now on I'll never wear a hat to a soccer game again."

That sounded promising, thought Sam.

"If it's under fifty degrees, I'll just stay at home."

Sam's mother appeared to be trying. Still, she didn't quite have the hang of acting like a regular mother. That same week she picked Sam up from her piano lesson in the Rustmobile.

That was what her parents called their second car, the old blue station wagon. Sam hated to ride in it. It had rust spots all over its body, like measles. The back doors didn't work right, so you had to climb into the front seat to get out. And if you sat in front when it rained, your feet got wet. Sam had the feeling that someday they'd be riding along and the bottom of the car would just drop out. Maybe then her father would get rid of the Rustmobile, but not until then. "I admit its body suffers from terminal rust," he said. "But it's got a great heart."

Sam couldn't believe it when she saw the Rust-mobile parked outside. What if her piano teacher looked out?

"What happened?" she asked her mother.

"Oh, I couldn't get the Chevy to start."

Sam slid down so her head was below the window.

"Why are you sitting like that?" asked her mother.

"So no one will see me."

"It's just an old car. It doesn't look that bad."

"No? Then how come Dad got that bumper sticker that says THANK YOU FOR NOT LAUGHING AT MY CAR?"

"It was just a joke."

After her father had put on that sticker, her mother had added one of her own: I'D RATHER BE READING JANE AUSTEN. Then Bradley had contributed ROCK WITH WROK. And Sam had stuck on I ♥ SOCCER. It was kind of fun to have a car plastered with bumper stickers. Except they made the Rustmobile more noticeable.

Sam felt her mother turn left at the traffic lights.

"Why are you going this way?" she asked. They would be passing the café where a lot of kids went after school. Kids like Bonnie and Betsy. And Brian Finnegan.

"I have to stop at the supermarket."

Sam raised her eyes to the bottom of the window. They were almost at the café. She caught a glimpse of blonde hair, book bags, Ash Can jeans. Bonnie and Betsy! She scrunched down again. Had they seen her?

Sam felt the car turn again, then slow down and stop.

"We have now arrived at the supermarket car park," her mother announced. "Would you like to come in with me or wait in the car?"

"I guess I'll—" Sam stopped. She noticed two boys walking towards the car. They looked familiar. Oh, no! It was Jimmy Humphrey and Mark Hartigan.

"Quick, read this." Her mother thrust a library book into Sam's hand. Sam held it up against the window.

The boys' voices came nearer. They were talking about baseball mitts. Sam buried her face in the library book. She hardly dared to breathe.

Arguing over the best way to break in a catcher's mitt, Jimmy and Mark walked right past the car.

"The coast is clear," Sam's mother whispered.

Sam looked over at her. Her mother was trying not to smile, but she couldn't seem to help herself.

"I'm sorry to be an embarrassment to you, Sam. I know a regular mother wouldn't drive around in a Rustmobile. I'm trying to be a regular mother, but sometimes it's hard."

Sam wondered if she really was trying her hardest.

So when Sam got the notice about the parent–child volleyball game, she didn't give it to her mother right away. Maybe she could pretend she'd lost it. Maybe her mother would never know.

But her mother got wind of it somehow.

"Isn't the parent–child volleyball game supposed to be on next Tuesday?" she asked.

"Uh – I guess so," replied Sam. "But you won't be able to go. It's in the morning."

Sam's mother always worked on her poems in the

113

mornings. She said she set aside her best time for her best work.

"Oh, I don't mind. It's not every day I get a chance to visit your school."

Sam had been afraid of that.

"Anyway it wouldn't be good for your shoulder." Her mother had hurt her shoulder trying to string lights on the Christmas tree by herself because Sam's father was lost in a maths problem.

"My shoulder has been fine for months. Don't you want me to come?"

"I *want* you to come," Sam began. "But—"

"I know," interrupted her mother with a smile. "You want me to come but only if I can act like a regular mother."

Sam couldn't help smiling back.

"Right."

"I'll tell you what we can do. You set down the rules for my behaviour, and I will follow them. Okay?"

"Okay," agreed Sam.

She went up to her room and lay on her bed, thinking. Then she took a sheet of paper and wrote down the rules.

Official Rules for Volleyball

1. *Wear your grey tracksuit.*
2. *Only hit the ball when it comes right to you.*
3. *Use two hands.*
4. *Don't show off.*
5. *Don't hug or kiss me.*
6. *Don't embarrass me.*

Sam's mother studied the rules. "I think I can live with this," she said solemnly. At the bottom of the paper she wrote: *I hereby promise to obey the rules set forth in this agreement. Signed, Carolyn R. Slayton.*

Seven mothers came to the parent–child volleyball game, and two fathers. Heather's father was there. And Rebecca's mother. And Bonnie's mother, dressed in a bright pink designer jumpsuit. Her nail polish exactly matched the jumpsuit. Sam wondered if she'd stopped off for a manicure on the way to school.

Mr Hagerty divided the class into two teams, with the parents playing next to their children.

"Here are the rules of the contest," he announced. "First team to reach twenty-one points wins. When the ball touches the floor, it's dead. I am the referee and official scorekeeper. Mr Speigel, will you begin?"

Sam wished Mr Speigel were on her team. He served six straight points before her team got a point. The sides weren't very even. Mr Speigel's team had all the best boys: Brian Finnegan, who was good in every sport, and Mark Hartigan and Peter Phelps. Sam's team had Kim, who was afraid of the ball, and Bonnie, who thought it was cute to miss on purpose. And Bonnie's mother, who seemed afraid of breaking a bright pink fingernail.

So far Sam's mother had behaved quite well. She had only hit the ball when it came to her, and she'd used two hands. And she'd been quiet about it too. You would hardly know she was there. This was exactly what Sam had in mind.

The score was 10 to 4. Marshall Tucker was serving

for Sam's team. He went into a big windup and hit a puny little serve. Rebecca missed it. Marshall served two more points.

"What is that boy's name?" Sam's mother asked.

"Marshall."

"Let's go, Marshall. Another one!" cheered her mother.

Sam wanted to sink through the floor. She flashed her mother a disapproving glance. "Sorry, Sam," she whispered.

Marshall served another point. Sam's team was coming to life. Heather's father turned out to be good. And Jimmy Humphrey was spiking the ball in the front row. Gradually they pulled ahead. But then Mr Speigel's team, with Brian serving, came back to tie the score.

It was 19–19. And then 20–20. Now Katy was serving for Sam's team, with a chance to win the game.

"You can do it, Katy!" urged Sam's mother.

Sam glared at her again, but she didn't seem to notice. Her mother's cheeks were pink and her hair was flying in all directions. Sam could tell she'd forgotten everything except winning the game.

Katy served. Mr Speigel hit it back.

"I've got it!" yelled Sam's mother.

She hit it across to Rebecca, who juggled it over to Mark Hartigan. He spiked it back at Bonnie's mother.

"Oh!" she cried, putting up her pinked-tipped hands. The ball bounced off them. It was going out of bounds. No one could reach it.

But suddenly Sam's mother was there. She spiked the ball hard, right at Brian Finnegan. It hit him in the nose, and he fell down. Mr Speigel made a desperate dive, but he fell too, and the ball touched the floor.

Sam's team had won.

She couldn't believe it. Marshall's mother was clapping Sam's mother on the back. Heather's father was shaking her hand. So was Heather. She was surrounded. And on the other side of the net Brian Finnegan was lying on the floor, holding a tissue to his bloody nose.

"I want to congratulate the winners of this hard-fought contest," said Mr Hagerty. "It was a lot of fun. And now, children, it's time to line up for lunch."

Sam left her mother standing in a circle of her admirers. As they got in line Heather whispered in her ear, "Well, that's one way of getting Brian to notice you."

Sam frowned. It wasn't the way she'd had in mind. Not at all.

When she got home, her mother was taking chocolate chip cookies out of the oven. "Sit down, Sam," she said with a big smile.

Sam dropped her books on the table and kept on walking. She couldn't face her mother right now.

"Sam?" Her mother looked bewildered. "What's the matter?"

Sam didn't answer. She walked upstairs to her room and shut the door. It was no use talking to her mother. She didn't understand. She thought she'd done a great thing, winning the game for Sam's team. In a way it had been kind of great. But in another way it had been humiliating. How could her mother make such a spectacle of herself? How could she hit Brian Finnegan, of all people, in the nose?

That was the worst part. Brian had had to go to the nurse's office and put an ice pack on his nose. Now he was telling everyone that her mother had ruined his career as a movie star. His nose would never be the same.

If Brian had ever liked her, even a little bit, he couldn't like her now. And it was all her mother's fault.

A note slipped under her door.

Dear Sam,

I guess you are upset because I broke the rules about volleyball. I apologise. I got carried away and forgot. Please write back. I will be watching my letter box.

Love,
Your bad Mum

Sam crumpled up the note. It wasn't really the rules she was upset about as much as Brian's nose. But she couldn't tell her mother that. Besides, if she had followed the rules, the nose problem never would have happened.

Dear Mum,

You're ruining my life. How could you do that? You made a promise in writing and you broke it. You always say parents and children should trust each other. Well, I trusted you.

Your troubled daughter,
Sam

When she heard her mother go down to the laundry room, Sam put the letter in her letter box.

Two minutes later another letter poked under her door.

Dear Sam,

I agree it is bad to break a promise. Here is the problem. You want me to act like a regular mother, and I am trying. But it is not always easy being invisible. I don't think it is the real me. All I can say is I'm sorry.

> *Love,*
> *Your imperfect Mum*

Her mother did seem upset. Sam felt a little bit sorry for her. Maybe she really couldn't help being so noticeable.

Dear Mum,

Well, you should try harder.

> *Your perfect daughter,*
> *Sam*

This time, just as Sam was raising the toothpick flag, her mother appeared.

"Ah, you're just in time for a chocolate chip cookie," she said.

"No thanks," said Sam.

"If you don't eat them, I will, and you know what that will do to my diet."

One thing she had to say for her mother, she

made delicious chocolate chip cookies. Sam couldn't resist. She sat down at the table.

"Have you given up on me?" her mother asked, looking sad. "Are you ready to shop around for a different mother?"

Sam nodded.

"Oh dear, I was afraid of that. Well, I do understand. Some other mother would be better suited to your needs. Do you have anyone in mind?"

"Well . . ." Sam hesitated. "Maybe Bonnie's mum."

"Of course," agreed her mother. "The obvious choice. Bonnie's mother always looks terrific. She wouldn't embarrass you in front of your friends. And think of all the shopping you could do."

Ash Can jeans, Sam thought. Two pairs, maybe. But suddenly she remembered how she'd felt when all Rebecca wanted to talk about was clothes and boys. Could it be like that with Bonnie's mother? Was it possible that all that shopping might get boring?

"Or maybe Sara's mum. She has that cute baby."

"Oh, yes, that's been another disappointment for you, hasn't it? You always wanted a baby sister."

Sometimes, though, Sara complained that her mother couldn't take her to places because of the baby. The baby had ripped up her maths book and she had to pay for a new one. And once she'd thrown up while Sara was holding her.

"I'm surprised you haven't mentioned Rebecca's mother. She used to be your favourite. You said she let Rebecca do anything she wanted."

This was true. Rebecca's mother let her eat sugary cereals and watch all the TV she wanted and stay up late. And she was always buying her presents. Sam used to think she was the best possible mother. Lately, though, she wasn't so sure. Rebecca seemed kind of spoiled.

"Well, maybe it's not so good to do *anything* you want."

Choosing a new mother didn't seem that easy. Maybe they were all defective, like Sam's mother.

"On second thoughts," said Sam, "maybe I'll just run away from home."

Sam's mother smiled. "I wonder whatever made you think of that as the solution to life's little problems."

Sam smiled back.

"I wonder," she said.

Dear Sam,

If you run away from home, where will you go? Would you consider taking me with you?

Love,
Imperfect Mum

Dear Mum,

Somewhere really warm. Like Hawaii. Or the Bahamas. Or maybe Tahiti. I might.

Love,
Perfect Sam

Eleven

An Interview with Dr Jerome Slayton

I interviewed my father, Dr Jerome Slayton, about his job. My father is a mathematician. He tries to solve maths problems. Sometimes he uses a computer. But mostly he uses a pencil and

Sam ripped the paper out of her notebook, scrunched it up, and threw it in the waste-paper basket. It was terrible. She sounded as if she were in third grade. She started again.

An Interview with Dr Jerome Slayton

I interviewed my father, Dr Jerome Slayton, about his job as a mathematician. Dr Slayton is not a medical doctor. Dr Slayton received his doctor's degree from MIT (Massachusetts Institute of Technology). When he got out of college, he had a card that said DR JEROME SLAYTON *on his apartment door. Everyone thought he was a real doctor, and one time some people banged on his door in the middle of the night because their baby*

This was even worse. All those *Dr Slaytons* in a row. And that story about the sick baby. How had that got in there? Sam dropped another sheet of paper in the waste-paper basket.

She was supposed to be writing an article for their class newspaper. Mrs Pinkney had decided this would be their big writing project for spring. The newspaper would have school news, feature stories, editorials, cartoons, even food and fashion columns. Bonnie and Betsy were writing the fashion column, naturally. Rebecca was reviewing Matt Moon's new movie. Katy was doing a pretend interview with her cat. And their class was going to do all the editing and lay-out themselves and print it on the office copying machine.

An Interview with Dr Jerome Slayton

I interviewed my father, Dr Jerome Slayton, about his job. Dr Slayton works at a research laboratory, in the mathematics department.

It needed a zippier opening. Sam's mother the writer always said the first sentence had to grab the attention of the reader. Also, Sam didn't know what to say after the opening. She needed more information. She had the sinking feeling that she was going to have to interview her father, Dr Jerome Slayton.

Sam's father was lying on his back under the sloping roof of the attic, doing something to a tangle of wires.

"May I interview you for our class newspaper?" Sam asked.

Her father laughed. "It looks like you've got me

cornered. Sure. But will you hand me things from my toolbox when I need them?"

"Okay," agreed Sam. She opened her notebook. "My first question is: How did you decide to become a mathematician?"

"Hmmmm," said her father. "That goes back a long time. Sam, would you hand me that Phillips-head screwdriver?"

Sam gave it to him.

"Just think," he said. "When I finish this job, we'll have a light outside by the barbecue. And guess what else."

"What?"

"We'll be able to listen to music while we eat dinner."

"That's great, Dad." Actually Sam didn't see what was so wonderful about it. She knew what kind of music he'd play. French-horn sonatas. But her father loved to do home improvements. He got all excited about them.

She tried to get his mind back on the interview. "Dad, can you tell me what kind of maths problem you're working on now?"

"Well, that's a little hard to explain. It has to do with variations on Kasalovsky's Theory of Quadratic Progression."

"What's Kasalovsky's Theory of whatever-it-is?"

"That's kind of hard to explain too. Oh, my, look at those cables. The insulation is all dried out."

Sam looked, just to be polite.

"Uh, Dad, back to the interview. If you can solve the problem you're working on, what would it be used for?"

"Well, it adds to the body of scientific knowledge. And it might speed up solutions to – oops, I lost my wire. Let me have the long-nosed pliers, Sam."

He disappeared into his tangle of wires. A minute later he emerged, holding up two of them in triumph. "Now all I have to do is connect these pigtails with wire nuts and get everything back inside the junction box. Just think, before you know it, we'll be dining to soft music under the stars."

Sam closed her notebook. It was clear to her that the interview was over.

"See you later, Dad," she said.

Sam looked over her notes. *Long time ago. Kasalovsky Theory. Scientific knowledge. Speed up.* It wasn't many notes for such a long interview. And she couldn't seem to remember how they fitted together. It was all jumbled in her mind with wire nuts and junction boxes and pigtails. Pigtails? Did they braid wires like hair?

An Interview with Dr Jerome Slayton

Kasalovsky's Theory has baffled mathematicians for centuries. Now Dr Jerome Slayton is working on the problem. He hopes to speed up scientific knowledge and

A zippy opening, but probably totally inaccurate.

Sam sighed. She was going to have to interview her father again. When he wasn't working on a home improvement project.

* * *

"Sit down," said Sam's father, removing a pile of papers from his extra chair.

Sam took a pencil from behind her ear. This time she was going to really take notes. She decided to start with her father's study. She could use some atmosphere in her article.

Her father's study was comfortably cluttered. That was what her mother called it. Sam would have called it a mess. But it was an interesting mess. It was crowded with bookcases, filing cabinets, a rolltop desk, a sofa that no one could sit on because it was piled high with mathematical journals. And all kinds of odd things: a clock that didn't keep time but demonstrated how early clocks used to work, a radio that her father had built when he was thirteen, a lamp made from an abacus, two of his old model aeroplanes suspended from the ceiling so they looked as if they were flying.

Her father leaned back in his chair. "So. To what do I owe the honour of this visit?"

"Well," said Sam, "I thought maybe if you showed me some of your work, I could understand it better."

Her father looked surprised, but pleased. "Why, I'd be delighted. It's been a long time since anyone has asked to see my work."

He took a notebook from a stack on his desk. "This is what I'm working on now."

The page was covered with tiny, scribbly marks. It looked as if a chicken had run across the paper with ink on its feet.

"Uh – what is it?"

"Equations. You must have had a little algebra in school by now. Doesn't this look at all familiar?"

"Not exactly." During their algebra class Mr Puccio had written a few equations on the board. But they were short ones, like $x = y + z$.

"Well, maybe you'll understand better if I show you some of my earlier work." He went to the sofa and rummaged through his piles of journals. "This is my paper on Rinaldi's Paradox which was published in the *New England Journal of Mathematics* three years ago."

The page he showed her looked just like the other one, except it seemed to feature more circles and arrows. They were artistic, Sam thought.

"You see, when I first approached the problem, I looked at it from a classic Euclidean point of view."

Her father appeared to be speaking in some foreign language. "Gaussian curvature . . . time-space continuum." But he was so enthusiastic about it – his eyes bright with excitement, his hands busily gesturing – that when he paused to ask, "Are you understanding all of this?" Sam didn't have the heart to say no.

Her father talked on animatedly. Sam tried to take notes. Only, his words seemed to float away before she could write them down.

When he finally paused for breath, Sam closed her notebook. "Well, thanks a lot, Dad. I really appreciate this."

"Wait, there's one more paper I think you should see."

He pushed another journal in front of her. Hieroglyphics. That was what his scribbles reminded her of. The ancient Egyptian writing that had taken scientists centuries to decipher.

"Uh, Dad. I think I hear Mum calling me. I have to lay the table."

"Really?" He looked disappointed. "Well, all right. I enjoyed your visit. I hope it was helpful."

"Oh, yes." Sam smiled brightly. "Very helpful."

An Interview with Dr Jerome Slayton

Dr Jerome Slayton leaned back in his chair. He was sitting in his study, a room where he spends a lot of time. Dr Slayton's study is an interesting place. Hanging from the ceiling are model aeroplanes that he built many years ago. Dr Slayton was crazy about aeroplanes when he was a boy. There are other interesting things in the room too. He has a radio he built when he was thirteen years old. It still plays, but not very well. Also a calendar shaped like a slide rule.

Dr Slayton's study is also filled with books and magazines about mathematics. This is because he is a mathematician. Three years ago he wrote a paper which was published in the New England Journal of Mathematics. *Right now he is working on Kasalovsky's Theory, which is*

It was no use. Now she had a zippy opening and a lot of atmosphere, but nothing else. This writing was hard work. How in the world did her mother do it anyway?

Sam dropped one more sheet of paper into her overflowing waste-paper basket and went to find out.

* * *

"Writing *is* hard work," her mother agreed.

She was sitting at the kitchen table shelling peas and reading a poetry magazine at the same time.

Sam was surprised to hear her say that. She'd thought it was hard for her because she probably wasn't any good at it.

"See this?" Her mother held up the magazine. "How long do you think it took the poet to write this?"

The poem was called "Ruminations on Time and Space, Albert Einstein, and a Speckled Brown Egg". The title was nearly as long as the poem, which was about eight lines.

"Two days?" guessed Sam.

"Two months, probably. Or six months. Or more. Let me show you something else."

She led the way to the spare room, which she used as an office. She pointed to the waste-paper basket next to her desk.

"That is my latest poem," she said.

The waste-paper basket was filled to the top with scrunched-up pieces of paper. Just like Sam's.

This was hard to believe. *Real* writers sat down and words just flowed out from their brains on to the paper. It couldn't possibly be the same for them as it was for Sam.

"Actually, that's nothing," her mother said. "Once it took me two weeks and four waste-paper baskets to write one single line."

This was crazy. "If writing is such hard work," Sam said, "why does anyone do it?"

"That's a good question." Her mother sat down in her chair. "It is frustrating work. You have to do it all alone. You can sit at your desk for hours and have nothing to show for it. When you finally do finish something and send it out, it's likely to come back with a rejection letter. And even if it is published, the pay isn't very good. And you probably won't be famous."

A writer's life seemed pretty grim. "Why don't you just quit and get a regular job?" Sam suggested.

Her mother twirled around in her chair. "Sometimes," she said softly, "after all those hours of trying, you come up with just the right word. Or phrase, or sentence. And then you have created something. Maybe you've expressed a thought that has never before been expressed in quite that way. And just maybe, if you're lucky, your words will touch someone else and they will say, 'Why, I never thought of that.' That, for me, is the satisfaction of writing."

Sam thought she understood. She wasn't sure it was worth it, all those hours and all those full waste-paper baskets, just to find a right word. But she could see that it was worth it to her mother.

"Now," said her mother. "How can I help you with your newspaper article?"

Sam explained about her attempts to interview her father. "What I need to know," she said, "is what he actually does at his job."

Her mother looked kind of embarrassed. "To tell you the truth," she said, "I've never been too sure myself."

Now Sam was in deep trouble. "My article is due tomorrow. If I don't hand it in, I'll flunk. What am I going to do?"

"Well," said her mother, "it seems to me that you have just learned two important secrets about writing. First, it is hard work. You have to do it over and over to get it right. And second, it's a good idea to write about things you know about. You don't need to flunk, Sam. Why don't you forget about your father's mysterious work? Go write an article about something that means something to *you*."

Sam would never have thought of that. She didn't seem to have a choice.

"Okay," she said.

Sam climbed the stairs to her room. With the rabbit sisters for company she sat cross legged on her bed. She thought for a while, nibbling on the end of her pencil.

Then she opened her notebook and began to write.

My First Baby-sitting Job.

Twelve

Samantha Slayton
6 Pinkney
Science Project

Problem: Which dishwasher detergent cleans best? Sparkle ($2.59 for 50-oz box) or A & P store brand ($1.49 for 50-oz box)?

Equipment: dishwasher, plates, bowls, glasses, cutlery, pans, food.

Hypothesis: Sparkle dishwasher detergent should perform best. The TV commercial says it cleans off burned-on food while treating fine china and glasses gently. Also, it costs $1.10 more than the A & P brand.

Procedure: I selected foods that would be hard to get off, like spaghetti sauce, peanut butter, egg yolk, and chocolate fudge sauce. I smeared these on all the dishes. To see how the detergents would perform on difficult cleaning jobs, I added a greasy frying pan, a pan with burned-on porridge, and a snack plate with pizza, tuna fish, and mozzarella cheese that had been allowed to harden for three days. I divided the dishes into two loads and followed the directions on each box of dishwasher detergent.

The science project was the last big assignment left for the sixth grade. The projects were going to be on display at the Science Fair in the middle of May. Sam wanted hers to be special. But she couldn't think of what to do.

"Plants," suggested her mother.

Sam shook her head. Plants were boring.

"Electricity," said Bradley.

Sam made a face. Electricity was boring and dangerous. Besides, all the boys were doing electricity.

"The chemistry of food," said her mother, glancing meaningfully at Bradley. He was cooking up one of his after-school concoctions again. It smelled terrible.

"Too hard," said Sam. "What are you making anyway?"

"A blueberry pancake with banana slices, brown sugar, garlic, and oregano," explained Bradley. "I've got it. You could test different brands of audiotapes and see which sounds best. That's a great project."

Sam knew why he thought it was great. He'd get to keep the tapes after the project was over.

"No thanks," she told him.

"Mould?" said her mother.

"Yuck. Anyway, Katy's doing it. I want to do something that no one else is doing."

Her mother sniffed suddenly. "Bradley, I think your pancake is burning."

"No, it's not."

The smoke alarm began squawking.

Sam's mother jumped up, turned off the cooker, and opened the window.

Bradley peered at his pancake. "Well, it's a tiny bit

overdone. The banana slices and brown sugar melted together. And the frying pan is a little messed up. Sorry, Mum."

She sighed. "That's my favourite pan. Your grandma Wheeler gave it to me before I was married."

"Don't worry, my good woman," Bradley went into his TV-announcer imitation. "This job calls for new Sparkle, the dishwasher detergent that is tough on burned-on food, yet kind to fine china, and leaves all your dishes as bright as sunshine."

Something clicked inside Sam's head. Here was her science project. She was going to find out if those TV commercials were telling the truth. She would test dishwasher detergents and see which one cleaned best.

"Mum," she said, "do you mind if I do the dishes?"

"Mind?" Her mother appeared to be going into shock. But then she pulled herself together.

"Not at all," she said.

"Okay," said Sam. "Dump on the spaghetti sauce."

"Got it," said Katy.

"A little egg yolk."

"Okay."

"A dab of mashed potato."

"Yup."

"Some peanut butter."

"Uh-huh."

"And a blob of baked beans."

Katy looked down at her plate. "Now, *that* is disgusting," she said admiringly.

"Now we smear it around."

They mixed and stirred and smeared.

"This science project is more fun than mould," said Katy.

"I think you need more egg yolk," said Sam. "And mush up the baked beans. Really cake them on."

Katy surveyed her work as if it were a painting. "It still needs a little something. What else have you got in the refrigerator?"

Sam checked. "How about some chocolate fudge sauce?"

"Perfect."

They dirtied up some more plates. Katy was really getting into it. She found a dish of tapioca pudding. And some Chinese food that Sam's mother must have forgotten about. It was green around the edges. Katy slopped them on.

She was creating new combinations of colour and texture. Not to mention strange, revolting smells.

"Isn't science great?" she said happily.

"I think it's time to start washing," said Sam.

They loaded the dishwasher.

"Eight disgusting plates," Sam counted. "Twelve knives and forks. Four jelly bowls, my mother's finest glasses. One greasy frying pan. One burned-on porridge pan. What's this?"

There was a blue ashtray, shaped like a star, that she'd never seen before.

"I don't know," said Katy. "I saw it, I smeared it."

"Now for the real challenge." From the back of the pantry Sam took out a plate.

"It looks like part of my mould experiment," said Katy.

"This is my brother's after-school snack plate from

three days ago. I've been ageing it. I have one from his friend Josh too."

It was caked with mysterious-looking blobs of food, including pizza, tuna fish, banana, mozzarella cheese, and what appeared to be a lump of bubble gum.

"That plate will be the true test," predicted Katy.

Sam got the Sparkle box. Carefully she measured out the blue powder according to the directions. She closed the door.

"Okay, Sparkle, the powerful dishwasher detergent," she said. "Do your stuff."

The dishwasher stopped humming. The little red light winked off.

"It's done," said Katy.

Sam unlatched the door.

"Hey," she said. "They're clean."

It was amazing. All that food they'd smeared on had disappeared. The plates were shiny. The cutlery sparkled. Sam held a glass up to the window. No spots.

"Looks like those Sparkle people know what they're talking about," said Katy.

Sam took out Bradley's snack plate.

"Well," she said, "it didn't quite pass the true test."

There was a tiny blob of mozzarella on the edge of the plate.

She checked the porridge pan.

"Or the porridge test either."

The burned-on cereal was still burned on.

"Uh-oh," she said.

Something very odd had happened to the frying

pan. All the grease was gone. But stuck to the middle was a big blob of blue plastic.

"What is it?" asked Katy.

Sam couldn't imagine. It looked like a fried egg. Only it wouldn't come off.

"The ashtray," said Sam. "That was the only thing that was blue."

"Hmmmm," said Katy. She held up the pan. "The heat of the dishwasher must have melted the plastic. Then it came into contact with the frying pan and created some kind of chemical reaction. Very interesting."

"It's not interesting," Sam said. "It's a disaster. That was my mother's favourite pan. We've got to get it off."

They stabbed at it with a spatula and pounded on it with a meat hammer. But the blue egg wouldn't come off.

Sam's mother walked into the room.

"Oh, no," she groaned. "My favourite pan."

"I'm sorry," Sam apologised. "We didn't mean it to happen that way."

She explained about the blue ashtray and the heat and the chemical rection.

"Ashtray?" said her mother. "Oh, you mean the sweet dish Bradley made in industrial arts. It started as a vase but something went wrong and it turned into a sweet dish."

"And now it's turned into an egg," said Katy. She looked at it critically. "It reminds me of those weird sculptures we saw at the Museum of Modern Art. Hey, maybe you could sell it to a museum. You could call it 'Breakfast'."

"That's an interesting idea," said Sam's mother. "But I think I'll keep it. And call it 'Sixth Grade Science Project'."

Sam was relieved to see that she was smiling.

Everyone was dressed up for the open house at Farmingville School: the parents, the teachers, the kids, even the school. A huge welcome banner, made by the first-graders, hung over the entrance. Totem poles, made by the fourth-graders, filled the front hall. The walls were decorated with art projects. And the classrooms displayed all the work everyone had done all spring.

Sam led her mother and father through the crowded hallways. And Bradley. Bradley was not dressed up. He was wearing his air-conditioned jeans and a black T-shirt that said RATT WORLD CONCERT TOUR on the front and had a picture of a disgusting rat on the back. And that same tattered hat that looked as if it had been chewed by rats. Sam was surprised her mother would let him out of the house looking like that. But her mother seemed resigned. She said Bradley was searching for who he was and the best thing they could do was say nothing about the way he looked. Sam hoped he would find himself soon. And in the meantime that she wouldn't have to go to many places with him.

"Here's my weaving." Sam pointed out a pink-and-purple place-mat in the display case on the wall.

"That's beautiful, Sam," her mother said.

Sam hoped she meant it, because she was thinking of giving it to her for Mother's Day.

"And here's my map of the ancient world."

Inside Mrs Pinkney's room Sam showed her parents all her book reports and the hieroglyphics they'd done of their names and the pyramid that three of the boys had built out of sugar cubes.

"And here's our Egyptian mummy."

At the back of the room lay the remains of an Egyptian king. At least that was what it looked like. Actually it was a plaster mummy that the whole class had made, using Jimmy Humphrey as a model. He had volunteered to lie very still on a table, covered with a plastic bag, with straws in his nose to breathe with, while everyone covered him with plaster junk. The mummy had turned out well, Sam thought. It looked just like the ones they'd seen at the Metropolitan Museum. Only a little fatter.

"Hey, King," said Bradley, tapping the mummy on the foot. "You're looking good."

To Sam's horror the mummy's big toe fell off.

"Yes, real good," said Bradley, picking it up.

Sam couldn't take anyone in her family anywhere.

"Come on," she said hastily. "I'll show you our Science Fair."

Mr Speigel's room was filled with people and science projects. There was a giant solar-powered windmill, a volcano that really erupted, a life-sized model of a person with all its layers of insides labelled, a disgusting dead bat, electric quiz games, optical illusions, a cage full of baby chicks that Jimmy Humphrey had hatched from eggs.

"This looks terrific," Sam's father said, his eyes lighting up. He loved science projects. "Will you give us a tour?"

Sam showed them Katy's mouldy bread. And Brian Finnegan's battery-operated racing cars, which were kind of broken because he'd crashed them so many times. And Marshall's computer betting game.

She almost lost her father there. He started asking the Human Computer questions and soon the two of them were deep in discussion of the laws of chance and Bradley said, "Well, maybe we can stop by and pick him up on Friday."

But finally she got him to look at Heather's plants. She'd grown flowers from seeds and put them in different rooms. In one room it was quiet, in another she played the radio on a news station, and in another she played rock music. Her experiment proved that plants preferred rock, Heather claimed.

Sam's father liked Heather's project. But he thought she should have played classical music instead of rock. "If you bring them to our house, I'll play the French horn for them," he offered. "They'll grow like giant beanstalks."

And then they came to Sam's science project. She had set up a display of detergent boxes, samples of detergent, and examples of the dishes washed in each load. She had clean plates, glasses, and cutlery, the unclean porridge pans, and the two Bradley plates. And a poster explaining her experiment.

"Very impressive," Sam's father said.

Her mother shook her head. "I wonder if I'll ever get the porridge off those pans."

"And look at that." Sam pointed to another poster, up in the front of the room. On it was mounted the frying pan with the blue egg. In large red letters Sam had written: AN UNEXPECTED DISCOVERY.

"Mr and Mrs Slayton? Congratulations!"

Mr Speigel shook hands with her parents, beaming. "This young lady is quite a scientist. I was so pleased about the frying pan!"

"Oh, yes," said Sam's mother. "Me too."

Mr Speigel didn't seem to notice her sarcasm. He was so wrapped up in science, than was all he thought about. This summer he was going to some remote island off the coast of South America to count sea turtles.

"I'm always hoping something like that will happen during our science projects," he continued. "It's such a good demonstration of how much scientific knowledge has been acquired by accident. Take Isaac Newton, for example. He might never have started thinking about gravity if he hadn't been hit on the head by a falling apple."

He went on, his big hands gesturing, his moustache quivering with excitement. Sam was going to miss Mr Speigel next year. She'd never had a teacher who was so enthusiastic about things.

Finally he thanked her parents for their help and went off to rescue Jimmy Humphrey's chicks from a baby who was trying to climb into their cage.

"Well," said Sam's mother as he walked away. "I guess my frying pan was a small sacrifice to make for the cause of science."

Suddenly Sam knew what she was going to get her mother for Mother's Day.

Results: Both dishwasher detergents performed well. All the dishes came out clean. The three-day-old snack plates came out almost clean. The Sparkle

plate had a tiny bit more mozzarella than the A
& P plate. Neither detergent was able to remove
the burned-on porridge.

Conclusion: You should not base your purchase on
TV commercials. The claim that Sparkle would
remove burned-on food was misleading. It might
remove some, but not porridge. The reason Sparkle
costs more is because they spend money on TV
advertising, so they have to raise the price of their
product. In this test it was shown that both products
are equally effective. Therefore, the consumer should
buy the cheaper one, the A & P brand.

_P.S.:_ Do not put dishes in the dishwasher unless you
know what they are made of. They might melt and
ruin your best frying pan.

Thirteen

Dear Mr Tooth Fairy,

Here is another tooth for you! This tooth has been loose for many months. I thought it would never fall out and then all of a sudden it did, right into my brunch-for-lunch at school. I hope I got off all the maple syrup.

This will make four molars that I have given you so far, plus eight baby teeth, for a total of twelve teeth. Isn't that amazing? And I think two more molars may be loose.

Your favourite tooth customer,
Sam

It was hard to believe there were only two more weeks left of school. Ten more days. Sixty more hours. And then Sam would be finished with sixth grade – and with Farmingville Elementary School.

Sam had mixed feelings about it. Part of her was excited, eager for summer vacation and then for junior high. And another part was kind of sad. Somehow she had never expected to leave this school, which was so comfortable and familiar. She knew every classroom in it, every teacher. The canteen ladies, the care-takers, the nice nurse who dispensed plasters, the cosy reading corner in the library, the clock that never worked in the gym. There could never be another place that would feel so secure. And yet it also felt too small. She had to leave it behind.

The last few days of school were always fun. No one did any work. They handed in books, cleaned out desks, brought home papers and projects. Sam was pleased with the projects she was bringing home. She'd got an A on her science project. Mr Speigel said Sam had shown originality and careful attention to the scientific method, important characteristics for a scientist. Sam wasn't quite sure if she wanted to be a scientist. She hadn't liked it at all when they dissected a calf's heart. On the other hand she'd really enjoyed working on her science project. Maybe she could be a scientist in some branch of science that wasn't disgusting.

She also brought home their class newspaper, which had finally been published the last week of school. Everyone thought Sam's baby-sitting story was funny. "Amusing and well written," Mrs Pinkney had written in the corner. In the hall, kids Sam didn't even know came up and told her about their own baby-sitting disasters. At the bus stop, little kids told her what they'd done to their baby-sitters. She was kind of famous. Sam liked this kind of writing. Maybe she really was good at something after all. A couple of things.

When Sam's cousin had finished sixth grade at the private school he went to, they'd had a graduation ceremony and he'd got gifts and dinner out at a restaurant and everything. At Farmingville Elementary School there was no graduation. But the sixth-graders were invited to a swimming party at the town pool.

This gave Sam a big new worry. All year she'd been wearing baggy clothes and layers of shirts and sweaters and changing her clothes only inside the cubicles of the girls' room. She was pretty sure that no one knew about her bra. But at a swimming party you had to wear a bathing suit. And you couldn't hide *anything* in a bathing suit. Everyone would also see that Sam's feet were deformed and her legs were several miles long. The day she'd worn shorts to school, when it was ninety degrees, a couple of the boys had called her "Too Tall Slayton". Wait till they saw her in a bathing suit.

Somehow too Sam's mother had got to be a chaperone. The class mother had called when Sam wasn't home and her mother had said yes when she knew perfectly well Sam wanted her to say no. Sam refused to speak to her mother for a whole day because of this, until her mother asked plaintively, "Will you let me come to your high school graduation? How about your wedding? Am I going to miss all the milestones of your life because I am a hideous embarrassment to you?" She sounded a little desperate. "Well," said Sam grudgingly, "I guess it's okay. But be sure you talk just to other mothers, not kids. And don't go swimming."

"I'm not a complete fool, you know," her mother said.

Sam was not looking forward to the swimming party at all. Maybe it would rain on Thursday. If it did, though, they'd just have it on Friday. Maybe it would rain for a whole week.

But Thursday morning was sunny and hot. A perfect

day for a swimming party. Sam packed her beach bag with everything she'd need: her towel, sandals, comb and brush, sunglasses, suntan lotion, and the extra-large Mickey Mouse T-shirt she wore as a beach cover-up. It came down to her knees. She planned not to take it off the entire time. Even though Sam wasn't looking forward to the swimming party, it was nice to be packing a beach bag instead of a book bag.

The pool was completely empty. Sam had never been there before when it wasn't full of screaming, splashing little kids. It was so quiet, it felt strange. Everyone kind of stood around, the boys on one side, the girls on the other, the parents under the trees where they were going to cook hamburgers.

Then suddenly Mr Speigel called, "Last one in the pool gets an F in science!"

Immediately Brian Finnegan did a cannonball into the water. Other boys jumped in, and they pushed in a few of the girls. Pretty soon kids were racing each other and diving and playing ball, and the pool sounded just the way it always did on a summer afternoon.

"Want to go in?" asked Heather.

"Not yet," said Sam.

"Let's find a good place to sit," said Meredith.

The four of them – Sam and Katy and Heather and Meredith – spread out their towels on the grass. They rubbed suntan lotion on each other's backs and watched Brian and Peter Phelps doing wild swan dives off the high diving board and talked about boys.

"Do you still like Peter?" Sam asked Meredith.

"Of course. But I think he likes Susie. That new boy Robert in Mr Speigel's class is cute."

146

"Ooh, not him." Katy made a face. "He's at my bus stop. He is such a jerk."

Katy thought every boy was a jerk. She wasn't ready for boys yet, Sam thought.

"No, my hair! No, my watch! Put me down!" Mark Hartigan, Jimmy Humphrey and Eric Johnson picked up Betsy from her striped beach towel and were carrying her towards the water.

"Help! Save me!"

Bonnie and Rebecca and Sara rushed over, laughing, to defend her.

"Looks like the Busy B's have been busy shopping again," observed Heather.

They all had the same polka-dot bathing suit in different colours: pink, yellow, turquoise, and lavender.

"They are *so* imaginative," said Meredith.

"Like sheep," agreed Katy. "Hey, it's really getting hot. Let's go in the water."

They all went swimming. Sam kept her shirt on, but when they started playing water polo, it stuck to her legs and dragged her down. So finally she took it off and tossed it in the grass. A lot of other kids didn't look so terrific in bathing suits, she noticed. Jimmy Humphrey resembled a great white whale. Other boys had legs like twigs. "The Human Toothpick," Katy whispered in Sam's ear, looking at Marshall. And from what Sam could see, a few other girls had been secretly wearing bras.

After water polo Mr Speigel organised a tug of war in the grass, the boys against the girls and the teachers. The girls and teachers won. And after that they had lunch.

Sam went through the food line with her eyes down, anticipating an embarrassing encounter with her mother. *Are you having a good time*? she would ask loudly. Or *Try not to eat too much junk food, Sam*. But her mother plopped a hamburger on Sam's plate without saying a word. Sam was astonished. Maybe her mother was finally getting the hang of acting like a normal mother. Maybe.

Sam ate lunch in the grass with her friends, and then the head teacher came and talked a few minutes about what they would be taking with them when they left the school and what they would be leaving behind. After that Brian Finnegan and Jimmy Humphrey started squirting soda cans at each other. They jumped in the pool to wash off. And soon everyone was back in the pool again, having relay races.

Sam was sitting on the edge of the pool, resting after swimming a lap of backstroke, when suddenly someone came up behind her and pushed her in.

She went under and came up choking, her hair in her eyes, her nose full of water.

"Who did that?" she demanded.

Katy gestured towards a pair of toothpick legs that were waving wildly in the air, attempting to do an underwater handstand. They flopped in the water, and a grinning face emerged. Marshall.

Well, it would have been better if it had been Brian Finnegan. Why was it that no one liked the people who liked them? Meredith liked Peter, but Peter liked Susie. Rebecca liked Eric, but Eric liked Betsy. Chubby Cheeks liked Sam. Maybe Marshall did too. But Sam liked Brian. And all Brian liked was sports.

Still, a boy had pushed Sam into the pool. That was something. She hoped the Busy B's had been watching.

It was hard to believe it when parents began arriving to pick up their kids.

"Everybody out of the pool!" shouted Mr Speigel. "The sixth-grade swimming party is officially over. I just want to say it's been a great party for a great class. We'll miss you next year."

Everyone cheered.

"But we'll see you in school tomorrow."

Everyone booed.

Sam said good-bye to her friends and gathered up all her beach stuff and followed her mother to the car.

But her mother didn't start the engine.

"Did you have a good time?" she asked.

"Sure," said Sam. She was surprised to realise that she had.

"There's something I want to give you." Her mother dug into the depths of her enormous handbag, searching for it. Her handbag was so full of junk, she never could find anything. "Where is it? Wait a minute. Here. Happy sixth-grade graduation, Sam." She handed her a tiny blue box.

Sam was really surprised. She hadn't expected any presents. This was a jewellery-store kind of box.

Sam lifted the cover. "Oh, Mum!"

It was a heart necklace. Only this one was gold with a delicate S etched in the middle of it, on a short gold chain. Sam could tell just by looking at it that it was real gold.

"Do you like it?"

"I love it! It's beautiful. It's the best one in my

collection. Oh, I can't wait to wear it! I'm going to wear it every day."

Impulsively she leaned over and kissed her mother on the cheek. "Thanks, Mum."

"I wanted you to have something special to remember the occasion," her mother said, hugging her.

There they were, hugging in the middle of the car park where everyone could see, and Sam didn't even care.

"Good-bye, Sam!" Mr Speigel waved to her, getting into his red sports car.

"See you tomorrow!" called Heather and Meredith, leaning out the open window of Heather's car.

"Good-bye!" Sam waved to everybody.

Her mother started the car. "Home?" she said.

"Home," said Sam.

Dear Ms Slayton,

Our records indicate that the number of teeth submitted by you exceeds our established maximums for normal human beings. If this torrid pace continues, therefore, I must consider reducing your compensation for future specimens, perfect though they may be. And I shall have to ask that you submit a certificate of authenticity from your teacher, clergyman, or best friend.

Two more molars indeed. This is ridiculous.

Yours for a quiescent mouth,
T. Fairy.

Paula Danziger
Divorce Express £2.99

Divorced parents can act worse than their kids!

You'd have thought after the divorce that Phoebe's father would have been more understanding about Rocky. Away from her mother, best friend and boyfriend, Rocky the raccoon seemed to be the only friend Phoebe had. And so what if he kept knocking over the garbage?

It's funny how one week everything seems miserable and the next, everything's good. Just as Rocky was facing a death sentence, her father changed his mind. And then on the bus Phoebe met Rosie, who quickly became her new best friend. From then on, the future seemed a whole lot brighter . . .

The Cat Ate My Gymsuit £2.99

Even teachers can be human!

Marcy Lewis hated school till Ms Finney arrived. The new teacher was interested in everybody and everything – even Marcy the blimp! It didn't stop Marcy hating gym, and using excuses like 'the cat ate my gymsuit' to get out of it. But it did help her confidence. Soon she could even talk to Joel without blushing a million shades of scarlet.

When Ms Finney got suspended for her controversial new teaching methods. Marcy knew she had to take action and fight this injustice. And thanks to Ms Finney, she wasn't going to be alone.

All Pan books are available at your local bookshop or newsagent, or can be ordered direct from the publisher. Indicate the number of copies required and fill in the form below.

Send to: **CS Department, Pan Books Ltd., P.O. Box 40, Basingstoke, Hants. RG21 2YT.**

or phone: 0256 469551 (Ansaphone), quoting title, author and Credit Card number.

Please enclose a remittance* to the value of the cover price plus: 60p for the first book plus 30p per copy for each additional book ordered to a maximum charge of £2.40 to cover postage and packing.

*Payment may be made in sterling by UK personal cheque, postal order, sterling draft or international money order, made payable to Pan Books Ltd.

Alternatively by Barclaycard/Access:

Card No. ☐☐☐☐☐☐☐☐☐☐☐☐☐☐☐☐☐

Signature:

Applicable only in the UK and Republic of Ireland.

While every effort is made to keep prices low, it is sometimes necessary to increase prices at short notice. Pan Books reserve the right to show on covers and charge new retail prices which may differ from those advertised in the text or elsewhere.

NAME AND ADDRESS IN BLOCK LETTERS PLEASE:

....

Name ————————————————————————————

Address ——————————————————————————

————————————————————————————————

————————————————————————————————

————————————————————————————————

3/87